T0099756

FREEDOM ROAD:

A Girl's Journey through the Foster Care System

By
Tami Mays

Order this book online at www.trafford.com
or email orders@trafford.com

Most Trafford titles are also available at major online book retailers.

Printed in the United States of America.

ISBN: 978-1-4269-3478-0 (sc)

ISBN: 978-1-4269-3479-7 (e-book)

*Our mission is to efficiently provide the world's finest, most comprehensive book publishing
service, enabling every author to experience success. To find out how to publish your book,
your way, and have it available worldwide, visit us online at www.trafford.com*

Trafford rev. 6/28/2010

 www.trafford.com

North America & international
toll-free: 1 888 232 4444 (USA & Canada)
phone: 250 383 6864 ♦ fax: 812 355 4082

Dedications To all caseworkers who pinch their faces at injustice to kids To all guardians of children's rights To all teachers who are sometimes a blessing and a curse To all single parents trying to make things better for their kids

Chapter 1

The day my momma died was the happiest and saddest day of my life. I stood at the graveside by that black casket with my 5 brothers and sisters. I was crying on the outside but inside my mind and heart screamed one word: free! We were finally free! Now you may think that it's awful for a child to feel that way about her momma. But let me tell you my story. Then you can judge for yourself._My name is Mary. I have been in foster care for years. We all have. My 5 brothers and sisters and I have been in foster homes ever since that day. But let me start at the beginning. Our momma, Lydia Anne Smith, lived with her parents. She was beautiful with blue eyes and blond hair. She was an only child who was pampered and given everything. She was that all American cheerleader, church going teen who everyone wanted to be. She was popular and lived life to the fullest. Then her world crashed. She found out that she was pregnant. At the age of 15, Miss All American got knocked up by her boyfriend. All of a sudden she had no friends because they shunned her. Her parents would have disowned her if it had not been for me. My momma was ready to give up on life until the day I was born. She, who had once been so popular, had no friends, was an outcast, and lived in a house with parents who weren't speaking to her. She said that she had contemplated suicide until she began to feel contractions. Later she would often say that my birth saved her life. I was born early in the morning. My grandmother watched me enter the world and instantly forgave my mother for her "mistake". I was named Mary Anne Smith by my momma. She decided to give me the name Mary to remind her that her Son Jesus came to forgive us all, even her. My earliest memories are those of my grandparents and their smiles. They transformed all of their earlier devotion for my momma to me. They kissed me, hugged me, spoiled me, and gave me everything they could. I reminded them of the innocent child they lost. I didn't inherit my momma's beauty but was cute none the less. I had blue eyes and plain brown hair. My momma went to work everyday at a hotel and then to night school to finish her GED. Things seemed to be going great. My grandparents were happy again. My momma was gaining back some friends and had graduated from GED class. I was a happy baby girl who basked in the glow of a loving household. But as I was soon to learn, happiness for Lydia Anne Smith never lasts for long.

It was summertime. Gran, Gramps, and I had just come from a picnic in the park. My momma was supposed to be at work but was sitting on the front porch when we drove up. She had her head in her hands and was crying. Gran asked her what was wrong. Momma said that she was pregnant again. She was 17. I was too young to really understand what was happening. All I remember is Gran and Gramps yelling and my momma yelling back. She stomped out of the house and didn't return for 2 days. When she did, she stated that she was going to move in with her then boyfriend, her GED teacher and the father of her baby. More yelling ensued because my grandparents refused to let me go with her. So I didn't meet my new baby brother Zachariah who was nicknamed Zeke until almost a year later when Gramps died. My grandfather died of a heart attack while working in the yard. He was the only dad I had known. I loved him very much. At his funeral my momma introduced me to a baby boy dressed in a sailor suit. He had red hair and gray eyes like his dad. I liked him from the start. My momma began to visit more often after Gramps died. She said that she wanted to be closer to Gran, her only surviving parent. Zeke and I would play quietly in the family room while Momma and Gran would go through boxes and reminisce about the old days. I loved those lazy afternoons and hated seeing Momma leave with Zeke. I still wasn't allowed to live with her because Gran didn't want to be alone.

Chapter 2

By the time I was four, my momma had 3 children: me, Zeke, and Sarah who was the spitting image of my momma with eyes as blue as the sky on a cloudless day and blond ringlet curls. By now my momma was living back with us. She had had a fight with Zeke's dad. She caught him with another woman. To get back at him she cheated on him with a co-worker, a.k.a Sarah's dad. My grandmother was at her wits end with all of us in the house. Or at least that's what she used to say with a smile on her face. She took in momma, Zeke, and Sarah only because my momma agreed to get her tubes tied and keep working. Later we learned that even though she did get a job, momma never got her tubes tied. She said that she wanted to be able to have more children later if she ever got married. Times were peaceful. Gran watched us while my momma worked. Zeke, Sarah, and I played in the huge backyard at her house. Gramps had put up a swing for me to use when I got older and we twirled on it for hours. Gran bought us a playhouse to have tea parties in. Sometimes when she wasn't so tired, Momma would play with us too. It was the only peaceful times I can remember having. We were a family. We were happy, loved, and enjoyed our youth. Things were going great. Then one day my momma gave us some news that would change our lives again. She was getting married.

By now my momma was past 21. She was still beautiful despite having 3 young children. She had attracted the head of a small business owner. He was tall, dark, and handsome. He had a nice home, loved going to church, and wanted to settle down. He and my momma dated for about 6 months when she announced the wedding. My grandmother was shocked of course. Not because the guy was black. Gran had friends who were interracial couples. I'm not sure if it was the wedding or the pregnancy that truly upset her. None the less, the wedding took place 2 months later. And soon after Thomas joined our family. Thomas had curly brown hair and big brown eyes. He was spoiled and cuddled by everyone who saw him. We enjoyed teasing him by tickling his toes and rubbing stuffed animals on his face to hear him squeal. We all lived together in his dad's home. He wasn't around much because of his business so we spent a lot of time at Gran's house. Once again Gran tried to get Momma to agree to tie her tubes. But Momma said no because she and Thomas' dad wanted to have more kids. And they did. Within a few years, Naomi and Adam had been born and their dad was dead. He had been working late one evening and was on his way home with some flowers for Momma. It was their anniversary. He was hit by a drunk driver. They say that he died instantly. Our momma moved us back to Gran's house. The old house was a sight for sore eyes because her husband didn't have much life insurance. His business took most of the money with it when it failed shortly after his death. Gran was beside herself trying to handle 6 children and our momma who was depressed after the death of her husband. Gran's health began to fade slowly away. It was as if we were sapping her energy. Our momma was working longer hours trying to make ends meet. She was 26, had 6 children, no social life and stressed to the max. She was unhappy and often yelled at us kids. I was old enough to try to help Gran by taking care of the smaller kids. I was in school but would help Gran cook, set the table, dress my siblings, or anything else I could think to do. Life was always hectic. Each year brought more noise and confusion as each of us got bigger and older. More and more pressures were on Gran whose health got worse. By the time I was 11 she was gone. She died in the night in her sleep. I remember thinking about how I would miss her. And I truly believe that a part of me died with her.

Chapter 3

Gran left the house to our momma. It was paid in full 2 years before her death. Her insurance money paid for her funeral and got us through 2 months of bills. Then times got hard. Our momma worked all day at the hotel and then worked at night at the bar on the corner of our street. I, age 11, Zeke who was 9, Sarah, age 8, and Thomas, age 6 all went to the local school by bus. The babies Naomi, age 4 and Adam age 2 went to the free daycare that Gran had enrolled all of us in. Our momma would wake me up before she left for work in the morning. She took Naomi and Adam to daycare. Then she caught the bus to go to the hotel she worked at. I would get Zeke, Sarah, Thomas, and myself up, dressed, and to the bus stop. We ate breakfast and lunch at school using the free lunch program. Then after school we would go home where I would start dinner. Although I was only 11 years old, I could cook an ok meal. They were simple like Ramen noodles with applesauce or microwaveable pizza rolls. Our momma got peanut butter, eggs, cheese, cereal, juice, and milk for free from some public office. Sometimes I would make peanut butter sandwiches, cheese sandwiches, and even learned how to scramble eggs in the microwave. When our momma got off work from her first job she would go pick up Naomi and Adam. Then she would come home. We would all sit down and eat whatever I fixed and then she would go to her night job. She would call to check on us when she could. She used to come back to do this until her boss complained that he wasn't paying her to "get exercise". It was my job to clean up any messes, do the dishes, put the babies to bed, see that all of our homework was done, and then make sure that we all got to bed. When our momma got off work 4 hours later I would hear her come into my room. I would pretend to be asleep so she would kiss my forehead. Sometimes she would whisper, "That's my big girl". I treasured those kisses and that phrase because they were the only thanks I ever got for all of my hard work.

As you can imagine all of that work is an extreme responsibility for anyone especially a young girl. Things got worse when my momma lost her hotel job for missing too many work days. She had had to stay home to take care of us because we all got the chicken pox. So momma got another job at a restaurant that was further away. It paid less but it was all she could find. Because she had to go earlier than usual especially during winter, she paid an old neighbor woman to take Naomi and Adam to school and keep an eye on us. The lady smelled awful cause she drank and smoked heavily. She would scream at the babies if they cried and smacked us when we did something she didn't like. We weren't used to such rough treatment. Gran never hit us. She gave us time outs when we were naughty. And although we had received spankings from our momma we only got them when we really deserved them like the time Zeke broke the front window with his baseball. Or the time that I skipped school to go to the arcade. I didn't get to play any games. I just wanted some time to myself. But my momma spanked me good because she said she didn't need any trouble from the law. The law was always our biggest fear. Our momma told us to stop complaining about the neighbor lady because she came cheap and was helping her. Besides she didn't want the lady calling the law. The law could get really mean momma told us. They would take us away and lock us up. So we stopped complaining. When the old lady forgot to take Naomi and Adam to daycare, I did it. Sometimes she would be so drunk we couldn't wake her. So I would walk the babies to school after putting Zeke, Sarah, and Thomas on the bus. If questioned by anyone at the daycare, I would tell them that the babysitter went to the store or was busy with one of us kids who were sick. These lies were from momma who told us to use them so the law wouldn't get us. Since I didn't take the babies to daycare frequently, the people in the school believed me. On the days that I would take the babies to daycare I would go straight home. I had missed my bus so I couldn't go to school. Once I had tried walking but a nosy lady down the street said that she would call someone if I didn't get off the street. Afraid of the law, I ran swiftly home. Going home meant that I had some quiet time to myself. I would read in Gran's old room. She taught me to treasure books. I enjoyed those peaceful moments when I could reminisce or escape into a distant land, sail the seas, or battle evil villains. These times were often disrupted by phone calls from bill collectors. I never answered the phone but could hear the annoying messages left on the answering machine. Worse would be when the old neighbor lady woke up. She would scream at me for doing her job. She used to hit me but one day I pushed her hard and she fell. So stunned was she that she didn't return for 2 days. I told my momma what happened but she beat me so hard that she left bruises. Then she made me apologize to the lady. Later, that evening after everyone was in bed, my momma explained why she had spanked me so hard. She was afraid that the lady would call the law. She needed her help. I couldn't keep missing school or the school would call the law. On and on she droned about the law and the reasons that I should do this and not that. So after that night I didn't tell my momma anything else. I didn't tell her when the lady stole half of her paycheck money to buy liquor. I just let her punish me for taking it. I didn't tell her that the lady beat Thomas with a switch for spilling his milk. Thomas was always a sensitive child and had dropped his cup when the lady frightened him in one of her drunken stupors. She enjoyed teasing him and had jumped out from behind a door. Thomas screamed, dropped the cup of milk, got mad, and called her an old hag. She was furious. So she beat Thomas and stomped out of the house. The marks she left on him lasted for a week. When momma asked where they came from I lied and said that Thomas had fallen out of a tree. Our momma screamed at Thomas for being so clumsy and said that it was a good thing the weather was cold because his long pants and long sleeves would hide the marks. Didn't want nobody calling the law, she reminded us. Life went on like that. Momma's screaming and spankings increased. She called us awful names and said that we weren't grateful enough. She told us that lots of kids would be more than happy to get the welfare food we ate and Salvation Army clothes we wore. When we longingly looked at a new toy another child had or asked for something, she would roll her eyes. We had a roof over our heads, food in our mouths, and a momma that worked 2 jobs to put it there. Wasn't that enough? So we learned not to look for anything, ask for anything, and be grateful.

Chapter 4

The year crept slowly along. As my 12th birthday grew near, things seemed to be getting better. Momma still worked two jobs but had a boyfriend now. He gave her money and this helped all of us. She would put the money in a jar under her bed. When she left I would take some of it and buy us ice cream at the corner store. I would also buy whatever we needed like toothpaste, soap, toilet tissue, etc. During the summer months while Adam was in daycare, Zeke, Sarah, Thomas, Naomi and I would use some of the money to play games at the arcade. Our greatest thrill was to turn on Gran's old sprinklers and run through in our shorts and tee shirts! Momma paid the neighbor lady to watch us but she watched television and drank all day. So we were free spirits! Life was grand or so we thought. Then one night our momma came home early. We had had a great day playing in the sprinklers. The towels we used were dripping on the floor, mud was everywhere, and we were eating ice cream bought with the money I had pilfered from the jar. Adam was asleep in his bed. Our "babysitter" was knocked out on the couch where she had been since noon. Momma looked as if she had been crying. She walked into the kitchen where we were laughing. All laughter ceased when we saw her enter. One glance at her face as she surveyed the mess I was going to clean up told us that we were in trouble of epic proportions. Calmly our momma asked us what we were doing and where the ice cream had come from. When no one answered she asked again this time raising her voice. Once again her questions were met with silence from 5 children who sat staring at her with wide eyes and open mouths. I remember thinking, "Oh God! Why is she here so early? What is she going to say? Or worse do?" Wordlessly, I got up and began to clean up the mess. One by one my siblings joined me. We had become quite a team by now. We did the laundry, cooked, cleaned, etc. Our momma said nothing as we did this. She sat at the table and watched. The only time she moved was to wave at the old lady who woke up and came into the kitchen. She saw Momma, said goodbye, and left. When we were done cleaning our momma lined us up by age against the hall wall: Mary (me), Zeke, Sarah, Thomas, and Naomi. Without a word, she grabbed a wooden spoon from the kitchen drawer. Next she walked towards the downstairs bathroom. With eyes that pierced like daggers she said the only statements she would make that night. "You little ungrateful wretches cost me another man today. Your daddies all left for one reason or the other and this one says that he can't be with someone with so many kids." Then she pointed her finger at me. I followed it to the open bathroom door. I marched bravely in where my mother began to unleash her fury. I tried to bear it with honor knowing that my brothers and sisters were listening. When she was done, she shoved me out, grabbed Zeke, and began again. I sat against the wall and sobbed with every part of my being. Zeke was thrust out and Sarah yanked in. Poor Thomas shook so hard with fear that he wet his pants. I put my arm around him to try to calm his fears. Our momma threw Sarah out of the bathroom, saw me hugging Thomas, made a ghastly face, and snatched him into the room of terror. I believe that Thomas got the worst of the beatings because Momma had always hated his sensitive nature. Thomas came whirling out and little Naomi went in. Adam was screaming at the top of his lungs by now. Afraid that our momma would beat him too I went upstairs to get him from his bed. When I returned to the kitchen, Momma had put the wooden spoon on the counter. She made herself a sandwich, went to her room, turned on her television and shut her door with a mighty slam. Wincing with pain, I gathered everyone to me. We stood in a tight circle and cried. I'm not sure how long we stood that way until I let go and fixed us some

11

noodles, hotdogs, and applesauce to eat. While we were eating I had a talk with my siblings. I told them that from now on we couldn't trust our momma. She was not our friend. Neither was the neighbor lady whom we had knighted "the witch". We had to take care of each other from now on. We made a pact and pinkie swore even little Adam who didn't really understand. I swore something else to them that night. I promised to always take care of them no matter what happened.

School began like any other that year. I was 12 now. Since my bus came later, I was able to take Adam to and from school so I got rid of the witch. She said that she would tell my momma that I told her to go until I told her that we knew all of her hiding places for her liquor. I threatened to organize my siblings into a hunting party and smash every single bottle we found. (We really did know because we searched her house one rainy day when we were bored). She paled, called us some nasty names, and left without looking back. Our momma was thrilled to not have to pay the few dollars a week to the babysitter. She was so happy that she bought me a brand new dress for school. I hadn't had a brand new anything since Gran passed away. I wore it proudly to school on the first day. Because I was in middle school now, it became Zeke's responsibility to put everyone on the bus. He loved it because it made him feel like the man of the house. Life in middle school was very different. This is something I learned very quickly. In elementary school no one really pays attention to you if you learn to keep your mouth shut and fade into the crowd. But I became a target of many kids because my clothes were patched, worn, and not name brand. My body was changing too. I began to smell more and wasn't sure what to do about it. Hygiene wasn't our strong suit. We bathed maybe every 2 or 3 days. Our momma never talked about deodorant or anything. When Gran was alive we took bubble baths and had lotion rubdowns. But those were luxuries of the past. Our momma spent more and more time in isolation and left us to fend for ourselves. A kindly gym teacher took me aside and explained some things to me. She even gave me some deodorant, lotion, and advice about bathing daily. I thought, *bathe every day?! How? I have laundry, dinner to cook, dishes to wash, homework to do, kids to take care of, and more! How can I do this too?!* But I simply said, "Yes ma'am." I thanked her and put the materials in my locker. I was afraid to take them home because Momma had begun searching our rooms. She started after she discovered missing money from her jar. This resulted in another round of wooden spoon beatings for us all including Adam. And I knew that if she found out I had accepted charity she would be furious. She hated charity. So I began a new routine. I would take Adam to daycare, ride the bus to school, skip school breakfast to wash in the bathroom, put on lotion and deodorant, and go to my first class freshened up. I wasn't aware of it at the time but someone was watching me. This someone would become my curse and blessing at the same time.

Chapter 5

We had always been pretty healthy kids. Except for the chicken pox, we rarely got sick. This was remarkable due to our lack of hygiene and poor nutrition. (I mean I tried to see to it that we had applesauce or vegetables but really what do you expect from a 12 year old?) The only time we went to the doctor was for our annual shots at the neighborhood clinic. We had state medical insurance so it wasn't a problem for Momma to take us. She would make sure that we were spic and span before we went. She said that she didn't want the doctor calling the law. We saw the dentist at school when the mobile dentist visited. Ironically, because we couldn't afford candy, we hardly got cavities even if we did miss brushing once in a while. So you can imagine my surprise when I got called into the nurse's office early one Thursday morning. I walked swiftly down the hallway smiling because I was getting to skip math class. I loathed math! As I entered the nurse's office my smile diminished and changed into a look of puzzlement. Standing before me was the nurse, my bus driver, the school secretary, and my Spanish teacher. They were all talking when I walked in but stopped abruptly when they saw me. After brief introductions by the secretary, I was informed by my Spanish teacher that she had noticed my morning routine. She was concerned about my skipping breakfast. My bus driver mumbled something about an unkempt yard and never seeing my momma around. The nurse mentioned a conversation she had with the gym teacher who had given me the advice and hygiene materials. The secretary wrote all of this on a notepad. Throughout all of this I stood aloof with a dazed expression. I was very confused. I didn't understand. *What were they talking about?* I looked down at my clothes. I had on my brand new dress that wasn't so new after 2 months of wear. It had a stain on the front where I had spilled chocolate milk at lunch. But it was clean and so was I. I had washed up and put on lotion and deodorant. The bus driver left after saying that he would be available for comments later if needed. Seeing my bewilderment my Spanish teacher came over to me. She asked me to sit on one of the sick couches. As I sat, still wondering what was going on she asked me why I was in the bathroom every morning. I replied, "I was washing up." "Why are you washing at school?" "It was easier to do it at school," I explained. "Why?" "Cause Zeke and Sarah use the downstairs bathroom while I get Thomas, Naomi, and Adam ready upstairs." "You get your brothers and sisters ready in the morning", asked the nurse. I looked at her and said, "Sure! I brush Adam's teeth, comb his hair, and help him get dressed. Then I make sure everyone else is ready." I stated all of this proudly because we were great at getting prepared for school. We were hardly late anymore and rarely missed school. I noticed that the adults were all giving each other strange looks. Then the nurse knelt down in front of me and asked quietly, "Where is your mom in the morning?" I regarded her carefully. My radar went up immediately. *Why would she ask that? Was I in trouble?* Panic arose in me. We were never to get in trouble at school our momma said. The law would take us away and we would never see each other again. I began to cry softly. My Spanish teacher put her arm around me and said, "Mary, you aren't in any trouble." Relief washed over me. I wiped my tears away and sighed deeply. Then I hugged my teacher and smiled. She smiled back and said, "We just want to help you, o.k.?" I shook my head and said, "O.k." The school secretary began asking me some more questions now. How many brothers and sisters did I have? What were their ages? Where did they go to school? Where did my momma work? When did she get home? I answered all of them without any reservations. Then the nurse asked if she could look at my arms, legs and back. I asked, "Um, why?" She answered, "I just want to see if you are growing right." I complied and she gave me a brief examination. Then she said I could go read in the library. I happily skipped to my favorite place in school. I was deeply engrossed in Heidi when my Spanish teacher came to get me. We walked back to the office chatting about the book. I ambled into the nurse's office and was met by a lady and a man I had never seen before. They said that they had come to pick me up. I stepped back and said, "I'm not supposed to go anywhere with strangers." My Spanish teacher leaned down to me and whispered, "Mary it's alright. They are going to get all of your brothers and sisters too." "Why?" "They are going to help take care of you." Without another word the lady came over and grabbed my hand. My Spanish teacher took my other hand. The man followed. They escorted me out a side door to a waiting white van. The man opened the door and lifted me in. I turned and glanced at my teacher feeling a range of emotions from anger to fear. She whispered something to the lady who nodded. Then she handed me the book I had been reading in the library, Heidi. With a trembling voice, she said, "Mary, I know that you must be feeling and thinking a lot of things right now. But remember two things. One, trust me. This is for your own good. Two, whenever you get too scared read Heidi. She had to go through a lot before she found her way. You will find your way too." Then she hugged me and closed the door. We drove to my old elementary school and went inside. We were met by the nurse. We went to a conference room. Twenty minutes later, the principal walked in with Zeke, Sarah, Thomas, and Naomi. Zeke looked mad. Sarah was confused. Thomas was crying and Naomi looked frightened. I put my arms around Thomas who quieted down as the principal told us to sit. When we were settled, he stated that some of the teachers were concerned about us. We weren't in trouble. The lady and man were here to assist us. We were to go with them and do what they told us to do. We all nodded and walked together to the van. At Adam's preschool the lady and I got out. We walked to Adam's classroom. He saw me and came running. The lady spoke to his teacher in the hallway. When we approached she smiled and tried to pick up Adam. When Adam cried she told me to carry him to the van. With all 6 of us, they drove to a gray building with few windows. We were taken to a waiting room with lots of toys. The smaller kids began to play. But Zeke, Sarah, Thomas and I sat at a table with the lady and the man. They asked us many questions just as they had at my school. We answered them truthfully. Then Thomas asked, "When can we go home? I'm hungry!" The man stated, "You won't be going home yet. We are going to talk to your mom first and look at your house." "Why," demanded Zeke who was still angry about missing gym and recess. "Because," replied the lady, "We have to do our jobs and make sure that you are safe and healthy." She stopped then because the man left to get us some food. When he returned we ate and then played with the toys and games. We never had so many choices before. It grew darker outside. Finally another lady came into the room. She motioned to the lady and man. They left the room for a few minutes. When they returned, the lady called us over to the table. "I have to tell you something. I want you to listen and then you can ask questions. We talked to your mommy. She knows that you are with us. Tonight you are going to go to some special homes to stay in for a while. The nice people in these homes will take care of you." "I don't want to go somewhere else," I said holding tightly to Adam who had fallen asleep in my lap. "I know honey but you can't go home right now." "Why not," quizzed Zeke who was turning bright red. "Your momma can't take of you right now so we are going to." "But Mary takes good care of us," wailed Thomas who was now attached to my side. "I know but it's not Mary's job to take care of you. It's your momma's job. We are going to help her learn to take better care of you." With that spoken she motioned to a glass window. The door opened and in walked several men and women. Instinctively, I gathered the other kids around me. I understood it all now. This was the law! They were going to take us and we would never get to see each other again. I wasn't going to let that happen! Seeing my response the lady came over. She knelt down in front of me and said quietly and calmly, "Mary please, trust me. No one is going to hurt any of you. You will see each other tomorrow. I promise." For some reason I believed her. I believed her promise. So I relaxed. So did the other children who had been watching me. Then she reached for Adam who was still asleep. I handed him to her and said, "If anything happens to him I will hurt you." The lady looked surprised but said nothing. She carried 2 and ½ year old Adam to a young black couple. The lady smiled at them and said, "I told you he was adorable. Just look at those curls!" The man of the couple took Adam from the lady. Without a word they turned and walked out the door with him. "No," cried Thomas. I grabbed him and held him close to me. "Hush now. It will be o.k." Another black couple came forward. They were older than the first. "Hello Mary," said the woman. "We will take good care of Naomi. I promise." I nodded to 5 year old Naomi who looked sad and fearful. She walked over to the woman who reached for her and smiled. Naomi smiled back shyly. The woman picked her up and hugged her. She and the man waved to us and walked away with Naomi. A young white couple walked up now. "We are here for Thomas." "No! I won't go," screamed Thomas who held onto me like wet underwear. When the worker lady tried to take his hand he hit her and ran into a corner. She went to get him again and he curled up into a ball and began wailing. She sighed and said to the couple, "Please just wait a moment." They nodded and sat a table. The worker lady motioned to two other white couples who were waiting. The first was an older couple who took 9 year old Sarah with them. The man who I later learned was a pastor shook his head and mumbled something about "demon possession". The other couple was thirty-something. They quickly took Zeke who promised me that he would be good. The worker lady kept trying to talk to Thomas who was still curled up in the corner. The couple who sat at the table began whispering. The lady rushed over to me and said fiercely, "Mary, please talk to your brother! Your foster family isn't here yet but you can help me!" "He's afraid," I explained to her. "He won't go without me." "Well, he has to. You are going with a wonderful single lady who only has room for 1 more child. He has to go without you." The couple at the table listened to our conversation. Then they rose. The woman spoke, "We've decided to take Mary and Thomas." "Yes," agreed the man. "We won't make Thomas any more frightened than he already is. Mary can share our daughter's room." Sighing with obvious relief, the lady exclaimed, "Great!" I walked over to Thomas who immediately got up and grabbed me around the waist. He screamed, "Don't let them take me Mary!" "I'm going with you Thomas. It's alright." I took his hand, picked up my <u>Heidi</u> book, and followed the couple out of the door.

Chapter 6

The couple led us to a blue minivan. Thomas and I climbed in slowly. The man drove as we made our way through unknown parts of town. "We are going to pick up our daughter Cindy," said the woman. "She is at a friend's house. She can't wait to meet you Thomas and will be very surprised to hear about sharing her room with you Mary." When we reached the friend's house, a 12 year old girl with short brown hair came bounding out. She climbed into the van, looked at us, and happily exclaimed, "Two?!" Her parents explained as we drove to their home just two blocks away. Cindy chattered away about all of the fun we would have and all of the things we would get to do. The house was an ordinary brick home with a front porch and a tree in the front yard. We climbed out of the van and went inside. Quickly, the man, woman, and Cindy gave us a tour. It had 3 bedrooms, 2 bathrooms, a den, kitchen, dining room, living room, and an attached garage. Thomas and I smiled. It was much nicer than our home. Thomas's room was painted blue with sports stuff everywhere. He even had a sports car for a bed! Cindy's room was decorated in pink. She had a bunk bed, princess mirror, and lace curtains. The living room had a computer that we were informed we could play games on. But the room that caught my attention was the den. Built into one of the walls were shelves covered in books! These people had their own library! Breathless I sat down with Thomas and Cindy at the kitchen table. There the man and woman went over some rules. Actually they didn't call them rules. They referred to them as guidelines, simple instructions to follow. 1. We can't talk to our momma unless the caseworker said so. The woman explained that the caseworker was who came and got us from school. 2. We would see our brothers and sisters tomorrow and then once every week after that. 3. We would also have visits with our momma. The caseworker would be there and tell us how things were going. 4. We would go to church, school, and behave at all times. 5. If we needed anything, all we had to do was to ask them (Aunt Lucy and Uncle Scott).Five simple guidelines. Did we have any questions? I glanced at Thomas who began to look worried. I knew why. We hadn't gone to church since Gran died. She took us every Sunday. So I said, "We haven't been to church a lot in the last couple of years. But we promise to follow the rules, I mean guidelines right Thomas?" Thomas eagerly shook his head. Uncle Scott smiled and replied, "That's o.k. Mary. You will like church. Well, I think that it's time for showers, baths, and bed." Aunt Lucy led Cindy and me to Cindy's room. Thomas went to his room with Uncle Scott. After everyone had bathed, we listened as Uncle Scott said a prayer. Then we went to bed. Cindy and I chattered like two magpies sitting on a farmer's fence. She was on the top bunk of the bunk bed. She told me about our new school, her friends, and the church we were going to. I confided in her about my momma, Gran, Gramps, and my siblings. She cried a few tears and said that it must have been awful for me to have to do all of that work. I told her that I had never thought about it that way before. Exhausted after the day's events I snuggled under the covers and grew quiet. We were soon fast asleep.

Friday morning I woke up dazed and confused. Where was I? Then it all slowly came back. I looked up to the top bunk for Cindy but she was gone. Thomas cried out, "Mary! Mary where are you?" I rushed across the hall to his room. I found him the arms of Aunt Lucy. A strange feeling came over me. I was supposed to comfort Thomas not her! Before I could say anything, Aunt Lucy saw me. She released Thomas and stated, "It is o.k. now Thomas. Your Mary is here if you need her." Then she got up, kissed my forehead, said good morning, rumpled my hair, and left the room. As I gave Thomas a hug a new emotion swept over me. She had understood and respected me! A few minutes later, dressed and ready, Thomas and I went downstairs and followed our noses to the kitchen. The clothes we wore were ones the caseworker had grabbed from our house. They weren't new but were clean because I had washed them 2 days before. Aunt Lucy was fixing 3 plates of food when we entered. "Good morning," she said cheerily and motioned towards the table. We sat and ate pancakes with syrup, scrambled eggs, sausage, and fresh fruit. This was a specialty because the only breakfast we were used to was the school's and cereal at home. "Where's Cindy," I asked. "She's at school. Her dad dropped her off this morning. Uncle Scott is a doctor. He takes care of elderly people at the hospital". "Do we have to go to school today," asked Thomas whose eyes were as wide as saucers. "No. Today we are going to do many things. We are going to enroll you in the local schools. Then go shopping for new clothes, eat lunch at a restaurant, and then go see your brothers and sisters. Finally we will come home for dinner. Tonight's Friday pizza night!" "Won't your boss be made at you for missing work," I questioned. I didn't want Aunt Lucy to get into the kind of trouble that my momma used to if she wasn't able to go to work. Aunt Lucy chuckled and answered, "Well, no cause I'm my own boss. I work from home on my laptop computer." Thomas and I exchanged glances. *Imagine that! A mom that stayed home!* Our day seemed to fly by. We were registered in our new schools. Then true to her word, Aunt Lucy took us clothes shopping. We each had a clothing voucher from the caseworker. But she spent much more than the vouchers were worth. She even bought Thomas some toys and me some books to read! We ate lunch at a nice sit down restaurant wearing a new outfit and new shoes. Then Aunt Lucy took us to the visitation center. Thomas and I waited with Aunt Lucy in the center's waiting room. There was a receptionist who checked us in, a television playing the Disney Channel, some beat up books to read, some old toys to play with, and a small cafeteria with some vending machines. Time that seemed to fly faster than the speed of light now trickled like a brook. Finally after what seemed to be eons later, Zeke walked into the door with his foster dad. We ran to him, hugged him, and made remarks about his new clothes. This scene was repeated as Sarah, Naomi, and Adam arrived. As we laughed, chatted, and hugged our foster parents had a meeting with the caseworker. Then the caseworker took all 6 of us kids back to a large playroom. She said that we could talk and play with each other for one hour. One hour! I sat my siblings in a circle on the floor and asked how things were. Zeke replied, "I hate it! I hate momma! My man said that I have to do chores and made me go to school today! This is all Momma's fault! I hate him! I hate her too! I wish I was with you Mary!" I hugged Zeke tight and said, "I wish I was with you too Zeke. But I'm not and you gotta be good. You promised me." Zeke snuffed and nodded as Sarah began to speak. "My family is nice just too strict. They have another foster girl named Lisa. She's 10. We share secrets and play games together." Naomi beamed as she looked at us. I could tell that the older black couple was taking could care of her. She said, "My new momma bought me clothes and toys and cookies! She took me to McDonald's and gave me some candy too! I like her!" I laughed and replied, "Well I'm glad Naomi. I hope that you are a good girl." Adam was sitting in my lap with his arms wrapped around my middle. I looked at him. He seemed confused. I asked, "How about you Adam? Do you like your new home?" Adam was a bright 2 year old who was usually well spoken for his age. But all he said was, "No! Wanna go home Mary! Wanna go home!" I patted his back as Thomas and I told the others about our new home. After hearing all of the reports, I concluded that Thomas, Naomi, and I had the best homes. Sarah's was alright just too strict with the pastor's family, and Adam was really too young to tell us about his. Not much time passed before the caseworker who we nicknamed Pinchface because she always seemed to be scowling, announced the ominous words: Time to go. In her generosity she had given us 2 hours after asking our foster parents for permission while in their meeting. Before we left the room, she explained that every Friday we would spend 2 hours visiting with our mom. Then she herded us to the door. Chaos soon ensued. Zeke had to be carried to his foster dad's car by one of the male workers at the center because he refused to leave my side. Naomi cried pitifully but bravely walked to her foster mom who hurriedly handed her a stuffed bear. This soothed Naomi's tears. I said a hasty goodbye to Sarah as I tried to unwrap Adam from my body. Sarah wailed loudly as her foster mom led her out the door. As emotional as all of this was I don't think anyone was prepared for Adam's response. He may not have fully understood the entire situation but he did realize one thing. We were not going home and he was leaving me. He continued clinging to me and screeching, "NO! Want Mary! Want Mary!" One center worker trying to assist asked, "Oh, you mean you want Mommy?" Adam screamed louder and yelled, "NO! Want Mary! Want Mary!" Pinchface pried Adam's fingers loose and another worker unwrapped his legs from my torso. I cried and tried to reason with Adam, "I'll see you again on next Friday baby!" The ladies carried a writhing Adam over to his foster mom. She spoke calmly to Adam, picked him up, and carried him out the door. I watched as her husband got out of the car. He said something to Adam whose screams immediately ceased. Odd, I thought as I glanced towards Pinchface. Did she see that? I shrugged, walked away from the door, wiped my eyes, and turned my attention to Thomas who I knew would be a basket case. But Aunt Lucy was holding Thomas. They were both crying softly. She glanced up and held her arm out to me. I crossed to her and enjoyed her warm embrace. I couldn't remember the last time my momma had held me like that. Wordlessly, we went to the van. As we drove to pick up Cindy and the pizza, Aunt Lucy asked me, "Mary are you all right? I know that it must be hard." I nodded and said that I was fine. I was thinking that I wasn't going to cry anymore. I resolved to be strong for my brothers and sisters. Later that evening while in separate beds (Cindy and I asked Uncle Scott to take the bunk bed apart for easier late night chats) Cindy and I shared our daily events. It had been a blissful night. We ate pizza, played some board games, and watched a movie. I asked Cindy if it was always like that and she said, "Yes, for as long as I can remember." After she fell asleep, I lay awake pondering the events of the day. I was filled with melancholy about Gramps and Gran. I was angry at Momma for putting us through all of this. However, another thought forced its way to the top. For the 1st time since Gran passed away, I realized that despite everything, I was safe. That thought made me smile broadly and lulled me to sleep.

Chapter 7

My first weekend with Cindy, Thomas, Uncle Scott, and Aunt Lucy was awesome! We played in their huge backyard, had a popsicle eating contest which Thomas won, and attended church without a hitch. It was just as fun and exciting as Cindy described it! On Monday morning Thomas, Cindy, and I climbed into the van. We had our backpacks, pressed clothes, and homemade lunches! All of this happened after a breakfast of toast, eggs, and fresh fruit. As we drove to Thomas' school Cindy stated that she had never eaten breakfast at school and only ate lunch if she wanted. We pulled up to Thomas' school. Aunt Lucy asked me if I would like to walk him to class. I shook my head no and smiled shyly saying, "You can if you want to Aunt Lucy." She smiled back, took Thomas by the hand, and entered the building. Cindy and I giggled and waved at the cute little kids walking past the van. I felt a twinge of sadness thinking about Zeke, Sarah, Naomi, and Adam. I wondered what their new schools were like. Aunt Lucy returned to the van. As she buckled her seat belt she reported, "Thomas is fine Mary. He didn't even cry." Satisfied I sat back and listened to Radio Disney. We arrived at the school a few minutes later. Aunt Lucy said, "I'll see you girls later. Cindy help Mary find her classes. Mary enjoy your first day!" Cindy and I walked into the building together. Although we shared no classes, we did have the same lunch period. There I was introduced to many of Cindy's friends. She called me her Cousin Mary and said that I was visiting from out of town. On the way to my next class, Cindy explained that she really did have cousins who lived out of town and talked about them to her friends. I thanked her for the cover that saved me from countless questions. Cindy chuckled and replied, "Don't thank me. It was Mom's idea!" I ambled toward class thinking: I love Aunt Lucy! At the end of the day we sat down to a dinner of spaghetti and meatballs with tossed salad and pineapples. Thomas babbled about his new friend in school who traded him some cookies for his cupcake at lunchtime. Cindy and I gabbed about our classmates and teachers. I had a new Spanish teacher who actually knew my old one! She said that she would tell her hello for me. Uncle Scott talked about how his patients were doing. He didn't name anyone specific but I was touched to hear him speak with compassion about the elderly people he cared for. Aunt Lucy spoke about the chores she had accomplished. I nodded in sympathy knowing full well the awesome task of taking care of a full household. After our homework was done, Cindy and I played games on the computer. Thomas and Uncle Scott played ball outside. Aunt Lucy was putting dishes in the dishwasher. I offered to help but she replied, "No. Go, run, jump and play. Enjoy your youth!" Thus began my first week of school. I attended classes, made new friends, and read every day. I had finished <u>Heidi</u> and was in the middle of a new book by Friday. Friday morning, before we left for school, Aunt Lucy reminded us that we would be visiting our siblings and momma after school. Cindy wanted to come too but Aunt Lucy said, "I think right now that it's better for you to play at your friend's house." School that day seemed to drag on. I was anxious to see Zeke, Sarah, Naomi, and Adam. I was also nervous. I didn't know if I wanted to see my momma yet. And I felt guilty because I was enjoying my new life of being a kid for once. Aunt Lucy came with Thomas to pick me up from school. He was unusually quiet. I noticed that he had on different clothes. Seeing my expression Aunt Lucy explained, "Thomas threw up at school today. I had to bring him a change of clothes. I think that he may be a little upset about the visit." As we pulled into the parking lot of the visitation center my heart leapt to my throat. Remembering my resolution to be strong I swallowed hard, took a deep breath, and steadied my hands.

Thomas looked like he was going to hurl again. He grabbed my hand. "It's going to be fine," I whispered to him. "Remember we are going to see Zeke, Sarah, Naomi, and Adam today." "And Momma too," wailed the 7 year old. Aunt Lucy, who was watching from the open van door said, "Mary, Thomas, I know that this is hard. But sometimes bad has to happen before the good. Try to remember that." Thomas and I nodded and walked into the building with her. Once inside we were mobbed by Adam and Naomi who had arrived 15 minutes earlier. "Mary! Mary! I missed you," exclaimed Adam whom I was now holding. Naomi was clutching Thomas's hand and yelled, "Hi!" The door opened and in walked Zeke who had a sullen look on his face. Seeing us, he smiled and yelled, "Hey guys!" Sarah came in wearing a smile and we all hugged. As we sat on the floor in the toy area I surveyed my brothers and sisters. Sarah looked bigger somehow. Her blue eyes sparkled in the light and her blond curls were springy. Adam, normally a chatterbox, clung tightly to me and kept glancing sideways at his foster dad. Whenever the man looked up from the magazine he was reading, Adam would duck his head. Zeke was wearing jeans with a hole torn in the knee and a shirt that had a rip in the side. His hair was matted and his face redder than usual. Naomi smiled sweetly to her foster mom who waved her bear at her. Naomi said the bear's name was Gumdrop. I was about to ask Zeke about his clothes when Pinchface the caseworker entered the room with our momma. An instant hush fell over the room. I never truly understood the whole pin drop comment until that moment. The silence was deafening. "Why hello children," said Pinchface. We mumbled hello without taking our eyes off of our momma. Lydia Anne Smith had on a simple white blouse and blue jeans. Her hair was done up in a ponytail. She walked over to us and sat in a chair nearby. None of us moved. Pinchface, our foster parents, and the rest of the world watched and waited. "Well children, aren't you going to say hello to your momma?" None of us spoke. None of us moved. I don't even think that we blinked. We faced our momma like 2 cobras circling each other. Neither of us moved because we were too afraid of being bitten. Pinchface led us to the large playroom again. We had walked behind her and our momma as if it was our last march. And I knew what we were all thinking. *What is she going to say? Do? What will happen now?* We sat on the floor in a semicircle facing Pinchface and our momma. After a brief moment of silence that you could have cut with a knife our momma spoke, "Well children. I'm glad to see you. I want to know all about how you are doing." She turned to me and asked, "So Mary, how do you like your new school?" I dryly responded, "It's fine." She nodded and turned to Zeke who was sitting at the other end of the semicircle. "I hear that you have been in a lot of trouble young man! What do you have to say for yourself?" So that explains it I thought as Zeke glared at our momma. He's been in trouble! I'm gonna have to talk to that boy! Getting zip from Zeke, my momma looked at Sarah. "So mini-me, how have you been?" Sarah smiled and answered, "Fine." Our momma then sneered at Thomas who was sitting next to me. "I hear that you had to be placed with Mary because you cried. You have to learn to buck up boy. I worry about people taking advantage of you." Thomas didn't say anything. He just looked at his sneakers. Momma turned to Naomi. "How have you been sweet pea," she asked sweetly. "I've been good. I don't want no law!" Cringing at the word law our momma turned toward Adam who was snuggling in my lap. She held out her arms and said," Come see me my precious baby boy!" Adam began to cry when she reached for him and protested, "I want Mary! I want Mary!" I held him tighter and rocked him while giving Momma the "try if you want to" look. Our momma glanced sideways at the caseworker who was saying something to Zeke. Then she gave me the "just you wait I'm gonna get you" look. Pinchface suggested that our momma spend her remaining time with us by allowing us (kids) to talk freely and play with each other without adult interruption. I heard her whisper, "You may learn more from that then through your questions." They sat on the couch as we began to move about. We spoke in low tones as we explored the toys. I chose to speak to Zeke first. "What's wrong with you? Why are you acting up?" "Aw Mary," Zeke began to say. "No Zeke! You promised me you would be good!" Zeke turned bright red and began to cry. "I know but it's not my fault!" Everyone stopped what they were doing as he continued. "My foster dad said that Momma was a whore and no good. I told him to shut up! He hit me and said that I was an ungrateful brat who came from a whore who spawned mixed breeds. One of his sons told the kids at school! They started calling me names! I got in a fight with one boy today because he said I was trash! I'm sorry Mary! I wish I was with you!" Zeke cried woefully as the caseworker pinched her face up more than usual. She called another worker into the room and left in a rush. When she returned I had quieted Zeke. Pinchface told Zeke that he wouldn't have to go back to that foster home and would be leaving with her so she could take him to another. Our momma who had sat back calmly as all of this unfolded, smiled ruefully. She folded her arms and said smugly, "He never got in fights in school when I had him. Yet they say I'm the one who's unfit." The rest of the visit went smoothly. Released from his burden, Zeke told Thomas jokes. Naomi, Sarah, and I chatted about clothes and school while Adam played with a truck by my side. Once as he lifted his shirt, I saw a bruise on his back. Before I could investigate, the caseworker said quietly, "It's time to go. Say goodbye to your momma kids. You will see her again next Friday." We said goodbye. Only Naomi and Sarah hugged Momma. Satisfied she smiled and half-waved to the rest of us. I carried Adam out to the waiting area. The man wasn't there. Relieved I quickly said goodbye to Sarah and Naomi. There were a few tears but not many. Thomas, Zeke, Adam, and I sat in the toy area while Pinchface made some phone calls in the next room. After about 5 calls, she returned and announced happily, "Zachariah, I have a new home for you. I will take you there tonight." I glared at Zeke who ducked his head and stammered, "I'll be good Mary." We laughed as Adam's foster mom came into the door. I watched Adam closely to see his reaction. He smiled and ran to her saying, "Auntie!" As she lifted him up I saw that mark again on his back. I breathed deeply and said, "Be good Adam." That was a mistake because he began screaming, "Want Mary! Want Mary!" His "auntie" tried to calm him by speaking quietly. She said, "No baby. Please hush! Hush, it's o.k. Mary will be back." Adam continued wailing as she walked briskly out the door. I watched as they approached the car. The man got out. Seeing him Adam went rigid and got instantly quiet. He clung to the woman's neck and wouldn't let go of her at first when she tried to put him into the car. I watched them drive away, walked over to Pinchface, and punched her in the arm.

Shocked, Aunt Lucy grabbed me before I could land my second swing. "Mary! Mary! Mary stop! What's wrong?" Pinchface looked more confused than hurt. I began to scream at her as she clutched her sore arm. "I told you that I would hurt you if anything happened to

Adam! Why does he have a bruise on his back? Why is he so afraid of that man? I'm gonna rip out your hair!" With that stated I tried again to reach the caseworker. Two center workers and Aunt Lucy were holding me back. Pinchface motioned for them to release me. She cautiously approached and said calmly, "Mary, I'm sorry. I didn't notice. There are so many of you to keep track of. But that's no excuse. I will check up on Adam after I take Zeke to his new home o.k. honey." Satisfied, I calmed down and nodded. Zeke, who had jumped up when I punched the caseworker walked over to me and placed his hand on my shoulder. The cheeky 10 year old grinned and said, "Now Mary. You have to promise me that you are going to be good!" His devilish grin and comment made us all laugh. After a lecture, apology, and goodbye, I joined Thomas and Aunt Lucy in the van. Aunt Lucy didn't speak for a long time. I was scared. Was she mad at me? Finally when we were almost home, she spoke, "Mary, I'm proud that you stood up for your brothers today. I'm not happy that you hit your caseworker because violence never solves anything. But I understand why you did. And because of you Zeke and Adam will get better homes." I nodded slowly. Tears of shame pooled in my eyes. They spilled over as we pulled into the driveway. Cindy came running out of the house. Aunt Lucy sent her and Thomas on ahead. She sat with me on the porch and asked, "Remember the story you just finished reading called A Little Princess?" I nodded thinking about poor Sara Crewe. "She was put in a strange new world. She lost her momma and thought she had lost her daddy too. She was made to work hard and was treated badly. But did she give up?" "No," I whispered. "No," Aunt Lucy continued. "She treated people kindly despite how they treated her. She did her job without complaining and it all worked out in the end didn't it." "Yes," I sniffed wiping my eyes with my sleeve. Aunt Lucy hugged me and whispered, "You are a princess Mary. Always remember that!" With a forgiven spirit and a smile on my face I grabbed Aunt Lucy's hand. Together we entered the house to join the Friday pizza night fun already in progress.

Chapter 8

I thought about what Aunt Lucy said that weekend. We watched <u>Oliver</u> <u>Twist</u> and <u>The Little Princess.</u> We talked about how Thomas was like Oliver, shy and sensitive. And I was of course like Sara Crewe. That night Cindy said that she sometimes felt like Sara too. "Why? You have everything." "I always felt alone like Sara because she didn't have any brothers or sisters. She was all alone." I sat up in my bed. I hadn't realized that I had something that Cindy could have wanted! She was right. I was blessed to have grown up with so many playmates even if I had had to take care of them all of the time. I climbed out of bed and hugged Cindy. "I'll be your sister always Cindy." "I'd like that Mary!" We giggled and whispered into the night. The week was a blur as I eagerly looked forward to Friday. I was curious to find out how Zeke and Adam liked their new foster homes. I entered the visitation center with a smile on my face. But it faded once I saw Zeke. He was sitting across from the caseworker and our momma. They were talking but judging by his defiant position, he wasn't listening. Seeing me, the caseworker came rushing over. She took my hand and led me over to Zeke. She said, "Mary, please help us talk to your brother. He's been put out of his new foster home because he won't cooperate." Momma watched us cross the room and stated loudly, "Why did you bring

Mary over here? I am Zachariah's mother, not her!" "Some mother!" I began to unleash my checked tongue fiercely. I felt that I had held my temper for too long. "Your 10 year old son doesn't listen to you at all because you were never there for him! Your 9 year old daughter who looks just like you sees you as a total stranger. Seven year old Thomas is so frightened of you he throws up every Friday! Naomi and Adam are only 5 and 2! They don't even know you because you weren't around for them either! And I can't stand you because I had to do your job for you and all I got was a lousy kiss at night if I was lucky! Let's face it, you gave birth to all of us but Gran was our real momma. And when she died I took over because no one else would. You don't even know us at all! We come to these visits to see each other, not you! But we are trying to change. So why don't you try too?!" Everyone in the waiting area sat or stood perfectly still. Momma walked slowly over to me, knelt down, and said quietly, "You're only half right Mary. You are correct when you said that I wasn't around much. I guess I was too busy working trying to make ends meet." She sighed deeply and continued, "But you are wrong when you say that I don't know you. I do. I'm sorry for what you had to do. I will try to be a better mother if all of you will give me another chance." By now all of the other kids had gathered around us. We looked at each other and nodded our heads yes. I spoke for us all. "We will try. Everyone deserves a second chance."

In the playroom I learned that Zeke had been sent to an elderly couple who had never had any children of their own. They expected Zeke to be quiet at all times, eat liver, and wouldn't let him play outside! Inside the house he couldn't watch television, was to speak only when spoken to, and could only read or do puzzles. What a prison! No wonder Zeke had tried to run away. All of this happened on Tuesday. Zeke was already in a new foster home run by an interracial couple who had 2 other kids. So far, Zeke explained, it was o.k. I also found out that my hunch about Adam was correct. The man had been abusive towards Adam and his wife. When the caseworker arrived at the house, Adam was locked in his room. The woman wept bitterly as she described to Pinchface (whom I'm sure lived up to her nickname) how mean her husband was. She said that she wanted Adam because he kept her company during the day. The caseworker removed Adam and had the man locked up. Adam's new foster family was an interracial couple who had an adopted biracial daughter. During this visit, our momma seemed more relaxed. She got on the floor and played with us. This time when it was time to go each of us gave her a hug. Wednesday of the following week, Aunt Lucy picked me up early from school. She explained that Zeke was at the foster care agency once again. This time he fought with one of the kids in the foster home because the kid said he was a freak with fire hair and cat eyes. Aunt Lucy sighed and sadly stated, "I wish we could take Zachariah too but we can't." I reached up and patted her arm. "It's o.k. Aunt Lucy. I know you would if you could." When we got to the foster care office, Pinchface came storming out the door. "Thank God you are here Mary! I can't do a thing with Zeke!" I followed her to a conference room. Zeke had tossed all of the chairs and was sitting on the table. He watched me enter the room. I walked over to him and pointed to the chairs. Silently he climbed down and picked up each one. Pinchface sat in one. Aunt Lucy sat in another. I faced Zeke without saying anything. I waited to hear what he had to say this time. He took one glance at my stern expression and mumbled, "I don't care what you think Mary! You don't care about me anyway. If you did you would see that I was with you. You promised to take care of us! You promised!" At that we both began to cry. *He's right1! I did promise and now I've let them all down!* Pinchface sighed wearily and threw up her hands. Aunt Lucy, who had been observing the whole scene, strolled over. She sat down between Zeke and me. "I want to tell you a wonderful story about a young boy and girl. They lived with their parents in the woods. One day the father passed away. The mother couldn't care for the children without working in the nearby village. The only problem was that the village was so far away that she had to leave the children early every morning and didn't return until late evening. The children had only each other and the animals of the forest to play with. The girl who was 2 years older than the boy promised that she would always take care of him. He promised to be good at all times. But they soon learned that a promise made isn't always easy to keep." Aunt Lucy stopped talking and sat back. Zeke inched forward and wiped his eyes. "So what happened to the girl and boy? Did they get taken from their momma too? Did they have to live in different homes?" Aunt Lucy smiled and said in a low tone, "The rest of the story is up to you and Mary, Zeke. You have to decide what's going to happen to you now. Mary did the best she could to take care of you. She did an excellent job for someone so young. But she's just a kid, honey. She needs someone to take care of her. And Zeke, she did keep her promise." Startled, I asked, "I did?" "Of course, sweetheart. Who made sure that Adam left that mean foster home?" "Me." "Who got Zeke to tell about his first foster home?" "Me." "Who was so insistent that Thomas couldn't leave you because he was too afraid?" "Me." "Who has been the mother of 5 brothers and sisters for years?" "Me." "That's right! Now, who deserves a chance at happiness of her own, a chance to just be a kid?" "Me." "Right again!" Aunt Lucy hugged Zeke and me. We laughed as she tickled us. I stood up and faced Zachariah Smith. "Look little brother. We both have to do our part. I won't make any more promises except one. I'm here if you want to talk." Zeke grinned and replied, "I won't make any more promises either except that I will try harder in my new foster home. It's on a farm. That might be cool!" "Pinkie swear," I asked remembering our night at the kitchen table. "Pinkie swear."

Zeke kept his promise. He would come to the visits jabbering excitedly about the animals on the farm and his new foster family whom he referred to as the "Ingalls". Keeping my promise, I always listened to him and all of my siblings as they described the events in their lives. Things were good at first. Our momma came regularly to the visits. She really seemed to try at being a better mother. But after only 3 months, she began to miss visits. When she didn't come, we were sent home immediately. The first time it happened we begged to be allowed to stay but Pinchface said no. The visits were for us to spend time with our momma and not necessarily for us. I began to love and hate Fridays. I loved family pizza night with Mom, Dad, Cindy, and Thomas. (Thomas and I had begun calling Uncle Scott and Aunt Lucy that after 2 months. It just seemed natural.) But I loathed going to the visitation center. I never knew what to expect. If my momma came everyone had a pleasant time. We chatted and shared and were happy. If she was a no show, we cried and went home bitter and angry. On and on for a full year, this pattern continued. We were on an emotional roller coaster ride that wouldn't end. During the year we changed in other ways too. I became a young woman like Cindy. We snickered about boys, attended parties, and dreamed of going to college. Zeke put on muscle from working on the farm. His temper flared less. The "Ingalls" had won him over with love, patience, understanding, and time. Sarah was in a new foster home with a young white couple who had a little boy and a dog. She was removed from the old one when she confided in me that the pastor was molesting the other girl. The other girl told Sarah to warn her. I was relieved that Sarah hadn't been harmed and informed Pinchface immediately. That moron went to jail too. Naomi's foster parents had nurtured her well. She filled out nicely and her hair had grown long with proper care. Now she wore thick braids that hung down her back. Adam changed into a brilliant preschooler with an impressive vocabulary. His foster mom was a teacher who even taught him some sign language! I even noted changes in Thomas. He wasn't afraid of everything anymore. He championed for the underdog in everything. Dad put him in karate where he had earned his blue belt. Karate also built up his confidence and stamina. I remember thinking after one visit that things weren't so bad. Zeke, Sarah, Thomas, Naomi, Adam, and I had safe homes where we were loved. We got to see each other every week. However, Lydia Anne Smith's bad luck gene seemed to pass on to her offspring. Ironically, the news was great for her. But it spelled disaster for the rest of us!

Chapter 9

Despite missing visits now and then, our momma had completed all of her court requirements. The judge said that she had to get a better daytime job, secure more affordable housing, and complete parenting classes. She got a job as a data processor. She, with the caseworker's help, sold Gran's house. She moved into a 4 bedroom apartment. She completed the parenting classes and the optional nutrition class too. So it wasn't surprising to her when the judge ordered the caseworker to start home visits. This meant that we would be visiting Momma at the new apartment instead of the visitation center. It also signaled the first step towards parent child reunification. In other words, we were going to be sent home to her for good! Pinchface explained all of this at our last visit at the center. Our momma sat on the couch grinning from ear to ear like a well fed Cheshire cat. When Pinchface stopped talking, my momma asked, "Well, what do you think?" Her question was met by a wall of silence from 6 stunned children. Even 3 year old Adam had understood the importance of what the caseworker had said. We were going to be slowly ripped away from our new lives and loving families like a band aid on a fresh wound. What did we think? What the heck did she think we would think? The caseworker said, "Why don't you kids talk it over among yourselves." Momma jumped up. "There's nothing to talk about. You are my kids! I let the law take you away but that's over now! I did what I was supposed to do. Now you are coming home!" Disbelief shown on our faces as I turned to my brothers and sisters. Adam, sensing the tension, began to cry, "I want my mommy!" Our momma tried to pick him up but he pushed her away. "No! I want my mommy!" He crawled over to me and asked, "Mary! Where is my mommy? I want her." I shushed him and asked Zeke what he thought. He looked me square in the eye and said stiffly, "I'm not going home with that woman! I'm staying with the "Ingalls". I love the farm". Then he crossed his arms indicating that he had nothing more to say. Thomas copied Zeke's posture and said flatly, "I'm not going either! I'm staying with Mom, Dad, and Cindy." Sarah also folded her arms. "I'm staying with my family and my dog too!" Naomi copied Sarah and announced, "Me too. But I don't have a dog." Nodding in agreement, I shifted Adam to my side and crossed his arms too. I took up the cause and informed my momma and Pinchface who were turning red, "I'm not going either! None of us want to. And you can't make us!" Our momma looked like she was about to explode. Her eyes bulged out and her fists were clenched. I knew that look well and thought back to the wooden spoon. However, instead of blowing a fuse, she stood up and calmly stated, "We'll see."

Although we still had 30 minutes left, Pinchface said that the visit was over. She asked another worker to watch us and escorted our momma out of the room. When they left, I whispered to the other kids, "We have to stand up for ourselves. I don't want to leave my home either. Let's make sure to tell our parents tonight. Then they will tell Pinchface and the judge. Then we won't have to go." We all nodded our heads in agreement, pinkie swore, and waited to leave. In retrospect I can understand how foolish and trusting we had been. We were young, ignorant about the law, and didn't know how the system worked. It was like playing a game. We had made a move. Now it was their turn. We would spend the next months making moves, watching our opponents, and learning the rules. If we failed there would be no rematches. The stakes were higher than anyone of us knew. We had to win because we stood to lose everything. That night Thomas and I sat with Mom, Dad, and Cindy at the kitchen table. We ate pizza and drank lemonade. Family fun night was put on hold. Mom and Dad had already heard the news. They were trying to explain the rules to us. Dad began, "I know you 3 are upset. Why don't we talk about this situation?" Mom nodded and added, "Let's talk in the living room. I prepared for this all day."

Prepared she was. She handed each of us a notebook and pen. Then she hung up a chart board. She had written questions on the first page. "I want each of you to read these questions. I wrote them down after I heard the news. I want you to write any questions you may have on your notebook paper. We will add them to the board. Then we can get the answers." She flipped the next couple of pages. Each page had an activity to do and write about. It must have taken her hours to do all of it! So began our Friday night. It continued into Saturday. By Sunday we were pretty proud of ourselves and felt lighter. We had filled Mom's chart pages and reviewed them Sunday evening. The pages looked like this: Page 1 Questions 1. Why do Mary and Thomas have to go? 2. What happens if we don't listen to the judge? 3. What if we don't like it at Momma's? 4. Can we change the judge's mind? 5. What's going to happen in the end? Page 2 Answers 1. The judge said so. It's the law. 2. We have to do what the judge says no matter what. 3. We should be honest about our feelings but try to do our best. 4. We don't know yet. 5. We don't know. Page 3 Going Home to Momma's Pros and Cons Pros-We will be living with our brothers and siblings again. Cons --We have to leave Mom, Dad, and Cindy -We have to change schools again --no more karate-no more Friday pizza night --things may return to the way they were before we were placed in foster care Page 4 Our Feelings Mom--I'm happy and sad. As a mother I am happy Lydia is getting her kids back because I would want mine too. But I'm sad because I love Mary and Thomas very much. Dad-Ditto to Mom. Cindy--I'm sad and confused. I just want Mary and Thomas to stay here. Thomas--I'm mad. I don't want to go! It's not fair! Mary--I'm everything: sad, angry, happy only at the thought of possibly staying here, and other things too. But mostly I'm tired. I want all of this to be over. The last chart page was the most important one we accomplished. It had this written on it: If We Go We will have a goodbye party. We will behave. We will write if our momma lets us. If We Stay: We will have a staying party. We will keep being good and be extremely happy. We will be adopted by Mom and Dad. That weekend, after pouring our hearts out, we braced for the following Friday.

Chapter 10

The next Friday Pinchface picked us all up at the visitation center. She drove us to our momma's home. On the way there she explained that a woman who was our guardian appointed by the court would be also at the visits. It was the guardian's responsibility to report to the judge. She went on to explain that our visits would be for 2 hours at first and then increased to 4. Afterwards we would have overnight and weekend visits. If all went well, we would be home for good. We traveled through unknown parts of the city. Apparently our momma wanted us to start our new lives together in an area we had never lived. Pinchface stopped the van in front of some red brick apartments. "Come along children," she said as she knocked on a white door. Our momma opened it and smiled. "Hi! Come on in. Take off your shoes!" Zeke and Sarah led the way. Then in walked Naomi and Thomas. I followed carrying Adam. We slid off our shoes and looked around. Next to the front door, on the right was a small bathroom. On the left was the living room. It had a couch, 2 chairs, and a wooden coffee table with a television on it. As we walked further into the apartment we came upon the dining room area. It had a simple circle wooden table with 4 chairs. Two more chairs were sitting off to one side. The kitchen was to the right of it. As I walked towards the kitchen, I spied some stairs on the right. I climbed them with Adam still in my arms. My siblings followed us. The adults were behind them. Upstairs there were 4 bedrooms and a bathroom. Two of the bedrooms and the bathroom were straight ahead. To the right of the stairs were the master bedroom and a smaller bedroom. Momma explained the room arrangements. "The room at the top of stairs is mine. The room next to mine is Sarah and Naomi's. The largest room is for all of the boys. The last room is for Mary. She gets her own room." We explored each room. Sarah and Naomi's room had a bunk bed and a white dresser. The boys' room also had a bunk bed. There was a toddler bed for Adam and two wooden dressers. My room had a twin bed and a small blue dresser. All of the rooms had mini blinds up to the windows. As we went back downstairs, Zeke whispered to me, "Where did she get all of this furniture?" I had wondered that too. None of the furniture was from Gram's house. Momma must have heard Zeke because she said, "A local church donated some of the furniture. The rest came from a charity." Zeke glanced at me. A charity? Local church? Who was this woman? After we got settled into the living room, the guardian lady arrived. She introduced herself to our momma and us. Then our caseworker left. The lady said that home visits were a no nonsense event. We were to be on our best behavior and listen to our momma. We all answered her, "Yes, Ma'am." After covering the basics, Ma'am (which is of course what we nicknamed her) suggested that we color for a while. She pulled out some paper and crayons and placed them on the coffee table. Then she and our momma sat at the dining room table to talk as she went over some paperwork. Thomas and Zeke began to draw pictures of their favorite cartoon characters. Naomi and Sarah drew a spring picture together. I gave Adam a crayon. He made circles on his paper. I drew a picture of Mom, Dad, Cindy, Thomas and myself standing outside our home. As I was sketching in the tree, Adam said that he had to go potty. I stood up to take him. Ma'am said, "No Mary. Let your mother take Adam. She's the parent." Momma smiled and reached for Adam's hand. He backed away and yelled, "No! Want Mary! Want Mary!" Momma turned red as Ma'am walked over. She gently moved me aside, took Adam over to Momma, and stated, "Adam, this is your mommy. She will take you to the potty." "No! She's not Mommy! I want Mommy! Want Mary! Want Mommy!" Afraid that he would wet himself, I picked Adam up and marched into the downstairs bathroom.

When we came out, Ma'am said, "Mary, you are going to have to learn that your mother is in charge, not you." She turned and stomped away. I rolled my eyes and stuck out my tongue at her retreating back. The other kids giggled. Our momma hadn't seen my actions and questioned, "What's so funny?" Everyone quieted and Zeke answered, "Nothing." After half an hour of coloring, Momma suggested that we take a look at our rooms again. I led the children upstairs as I glanced at the watch Mom and Dad had presented me with on Christmas morning. We still had one hour left in the visit. We went to Naomi and Sarah's room first. It was small but nice. Sarah and Naomi sat on the bottom bunk. Thomas and Zeke climbed up to the top. I sat on the floor with Adam. "This is an o.k. place," remarked Sarah who was 11 now. "Yeah, it's not so bad," agreed 7 year old Naomi. "Let's go to our room next," suggested 12 year old Zeke. We ambled around the corner to the boys' room. Everyone took up their previous positions. "Well it's not home," stated 8 year old Thomas. "But Mom said to try to like it." Zeke leaned over the edge of the top bunk. "Your mom is really nice Mary. She made us funny face cookies at our last visit." He lay on his back and sighed. "My mom's nice too." I nodded as Naomi asked, "What do you want to do now?" Before anyone could answer our momma stomped in. "What do you think you are doing? Get off those beds this instant! Don't be thinking that you are going to be jumping off my new furniture and acting up! Move!" She pointed towards the door. We hurriedly got off the beds and went downstairs. Ma'am was sipping some coffee. She listened sympathetically as Momma informed her that we were upstairs acting up. "No we weren't," protested Zeke. "Don't backtalk your momma boy, what's your name? Oh, yeah, the troublemaker, Zeke. Now apologize!" "For what? I didn't do anything!" "Apologize for being rude to your momma. Now!" I saw the look that came over Zeke's face. It went immediately from surprise to anger. I completely understood but not wanting problems on our first visit I whispered, "Remember what Mom said." Zeke looked at me and said, "I know what Aunt Lucy said but...." I smiled at him. Zeke's anger faded. He mumbled, "I'm sorry." "Who the hell is Aunt Lucy," Momma demanded. "She's my mom," Thomas stated proudly. "I'm your momma boy not some foster person!" She turned to Ma'am, shook her head, and yelled, "You see! You see what I'm talking about? These people have poisoned my own kids against me! I did everything I could for them! But it was never enough! Then these folk come along with their fancy cars and give them the world! They have spoiled these kids for more than a year! Now look at them! What am I supposed to do with them now?!" Ma'am stood up and stomped over to her. "You just keep on doing what you have been doing." Turning to us she lectured, "I think that your mother is right! She's trying really hard to do right by you but all of you are ungrateful. The next time we have a visit I want no more mention of Aunt Linda or whatever her name is. And nothing else about I want my mommy either!" She pointed at Adam when she said that. "You will respect your momma, behave, and get used to being back home again. This is your home, your real home!" As she sighed deeply, Zeke mumbled, "It's not my real home." The rest of the visit ended without anymore mishaps. After a dinner of frozen pizza and Kool Aid, all of us kids sat in my room on the floor. "I think that we should tell our moms and dads that we didn't like it here," said Thomas. We all agreed. "I never thought I would say this but I wish Pinchface was here," Zeke said. "Shush," I whispered as I heard footsteps on the staircase. Our momma came in, huffed, and mumbled, "Ugh! Do you always have to do everything together? Come on. It's time for you to go." Six children rushed past her. As I walked past, she collared me and hissed, "Listen up you little heifer! You'd better learn real fast that I'm the boss in this house! Not your Aunt Lucy and definitely not you!" She released me, smiled sweetly and said, "Bye." Pinchface was standing at the door. "My goodness! I don't ever think that I've seen them move this fast before! So how did the visit go?" Ma'am smiled at us and lied. "They are quite a handful especially the 2 oldest. But I think that they will be fine once they are home for good. I'm going to ask for a speedy return home. These kids are too attached to their foster parents! The sooner they are reunified with their mother the better!" The caseworker motioned for us to go out of the door. "Well it's understandable that they would be attached. It has been more than a year!" "Yeah well, I don't like it! I've seen many cases but not one in which all of the children are so close to their foster parents year or no year!" Pinchface lived up to her name by screwing up her eyes. She bid the guardian a hasty farewell and loaded us up into the van. As the van pulled away, she sighed and questioned, "O.k. Mary. What happened?" I filled her in on all of the details. Oddly I left out my momma's mean comment to me. I guess I didn't want the other kids to worry. Zeke folded his arms and said, "I'm not going back!" Oh honey, you have to! I know it was hard today but give it some time! Things will get better!" But she was wrong. Things got worse.

Chapter 11

At the third home visit, our momma introduced us to her boyfriend. He kept saying that Momma was too beautiful to have given birth to so many brats. Once I overheard him ask which boy was the wimp. Our momma pointed to Thomas. He said, "I know how to toughen him up." He tried to make Thomas a "man" by wrestling with him. The result was a man-sized bruise on Thomas' back when the big idiot slammed him on the floor. The boyfriend didn't like Zeke saying that he needed a good dose of belt. He tried to give him this when Zeke punched him after seeing Thomas get hurt. Our momma intervened before he could land the first hit. The boyfriend called Adam a crybaby and Naomi a spoiled, pampered brat. The only child he was semi-nice to was Sarah who he said reminded him of Momma. But I didn't like the looks he gave Sarah and kept her away from him. So it was no surprise to me that the kid he despised the most was yours truly. He saw me as a smart aleck, meddling, busybody who stirred up trouble for our momma. On one visit, when Ma'am was getting something from her car, he sneered, "It's your fault you know Mary. You were the one who told the people at school about your momma." "I'm glad I did! She wasn't taking good care of me or my brothers and sisters! I did all of the work!" "Why you little..," our momma started to say. She was cut short when Ma'am opened the door. Momma smiled sweetly and said, "You kids need to be nice to my boyfriend. He may be your daddy one day." "Not my daddy," mumbled Zeke. Momma followed the rules so the visits were increased from 2 hours to 4 hours after one month. My favorite rule was that we could play at the neighborhood park as long as our momma went too. She would sit on the bench and chat on her cell phone with her boyfriend while we played. Ma'am no longer had to be at every visit. The caseworker said that all she had to do was check up on us and then she could leave us alone. What she wasn't aware of is that Ma'am had been leaving us alone with Momma long before the increase in hours. She said that Momma needed time to bond with us without outside interference. I think that she needed time to get her nails done because when she returned her polish would still be wet.

One particular visit, while at the park, Zeke announced, "My dad told me something about the law last night." We gathered at the top of the jungle gym play set. I glanced at Adam who was digging in the dirt. Then I looked at Momma to see if the coast was clear. She had her phone glued to her ear and her back to us. I nodded to Zeke who continued, "Did you know that a court date is coming?" "That ain't news man! We all know that," said Thomas. We nodded. We knew quite a bit about the law. We had been secretly learning about it ever since the first home visits. We knew that our foster parents couldn't say anything negative about our visits and were to encourage us to attend. They knew we were miserable but couldn't do anything about it. Zeke playfully punched Thomas, "I'm not finished. I mean that there is a court date coming up soon. I think that we are going to start staying here overnight. But they might give us a chance to talk to the judge!" "Really, how," I questioned. "I'm not sure Mary. But we might be able to. Maybe I can get Dad to tell me more. Uh oh! Shush! Here she comes!" Our momma walked towards us. "Alright let's go! I don't know why I bother bringing you to the park if all you are going to do is sit around in a huddle. You can do that at home!" I took Adam's hand and began walking toward the apartment. Momma grabbed him, pushed me away, and yelled, "I told you little girl, I'm the momma!" When Adam protested she yanked his arm and hissed, "Shut up! Ain't nobody hurting you crybaby!" Zeke, Sarah, and I walked together after them. "I wish Adam would kick her," Zeke said. "I tried to teach him how but he said that his mommy says to be nice and don't hit. His mom's cool but she's brainwashed the kid. He has to learn to stand up for himself." I laughed. Our momma shoved Thomas and Naomi ahead of her. Looking back she screamed, "Come on! I gotta feed you brats now!" I looked at my watch. She was right. She had only 30 minutes left to feed us before the visit ended. Dinner was hot dogs and mixed vegetables from a can. After we ate, Momma grabbed the remote and ordered, "Mary you wash the dishes. Zachariah you dry. The rest of you sit on the floor." "What are we going to watch," asked Sarah. "I don't know yet. Be quiet and let me find something." She turned to the animal channel. There was a show about elephants. As Zeke and I finished the dishes, our caseworker and guardian walked into the house. "An educational television show! How wonderful! Great job Lydia," said Witch #2 formerly Ma'am. We decided to change her name a month ago because she reminded us of the first witch, someone else who had been appointed to take care of us and failed. Zeke had wanted to name her Goblin but was outvoted. "I thought that you guys were going to play board games," inquired our caseworker. She pointed to the games Mom had sent over a few weeks ago. Momma stood up, stretched and stated with a yawn, "I'm not going to be continually entertaining these kids. If they want to play board games they can. I'm not stopping them." Actually she was. We had been warned to stay off the furniture and not mess up the carpet. Where else were we to play a game?! Saying nothing else, with a plastered on smile, our caseworker spoke, "Let's go children. Say goodbye." We mumbled goodbye and raced towards the van.

Once inside the van our caseworker announced, "Next weekend you are going to be staying overnight at your momma's house. I've already told your foster parents about it. I'll drop you off on Friday and pick you up Saturday evening." "What if we don't want to do it," asked Zeke. I jabbed him in his side. When will that boy learn to control his mouth! "You have to Zeke. The judge said so." "I wanna talk to the judge," said Sarah. "Me too," said Naomi. "Isn't it in the rules?" I glared at both of them and they shut their mouths. Jeez, couldn't they control their traps either? "Who told you that," demanded Pinchface who looked angry now. "Our momma," I answered sweetly. "Mary, don't lie to me." "I'm not lying. Our momma did say that. Once when we complained, she said, 'If you don't like it, tell it to the judge! I don't want to hear it!'"

Pinchface stared at me for a long time. The light was red. *Please turn green, please turn green!* It did and honks from behind made her continue driving. *Whew! That was close!* Back at the center, I glared at the three stooges: Zeke, Naomi, and Sarah who had almost blown our secret. They all looked glum and mumbled, "Sorry Mary," as they walked to their waiting Moms and Dads. I smiled, hugged each one, and stated, "That's alright. See you next week!" On the way home I thought about what Zeke said. I asked, "Mom is it true that we may be able to tell the judge that we want to stay with you and Dad?" Mom glanced into the rearview mirror. "Well, yes. Dad and I have been doing research to learn more about what the law says. But remember what I told you Mary. The law is the law and we have to follow it even if we don't like it or think that it's unfair." That Saturday night, after Mom and Dad went to bed, Thomas came into our room. Cindy and I were waiting. "I've been thinking guys," I said. "If we can talk to the judge maybe we don't have to leave." "I hope so. I don't want you to go," said Cindy giving me a hug. "If not, I have a plan B," I replied. "What is it," asked Thomas. "Not yet little brother. Let's see what happens first." As I lay in my bed I thought about plan B. I got the idea from the story Harriet the Spy. The kids didn't like what Harriet wrote about them in her notebook. So they banded together and got revenge on her. I had some ideas of how to be heard if the judge refused to listen. They would be the craftiest moves we would make in this game. We too would band together and make ourselves heard.

Chapter 12

The first strategic move began on our first overnight visit. Momma yelled at us for every little thing we did. We couldn't breathe deep without hearing her mouth. She had placed us in our various rooms on Friday night as a punishment for talking back to her when we complained about having frozen pizza again. I waited until she went downstairs. When I heard the television come on, I tweeted like a bird. Sarah and Naomi tiptoed into the boy's room. I leaned over the low wall connected to the staircase and listened. Our momma was watching some Friday night special movie. I walked into the room and whispered, "O.k. guys. I think that frozen pizza stinks too. But we shouldn't complain. It just makes her mad." "Yeah, well I'm sick of it anyway," complained Zeke. "We can't play our games. We can't go outside. We can't even watch tv. All we do is sit in our rooms all day. I'm sick of it! I'm bored!" "Me too," whined Sarah and Naomi. I nodded in agreement as I laid Adam on his bed. Thomas looked up from the book he was reading. "I guess we had better get used to it," he replied. "That's right you little ingrates!" We gasped as we turned to look at our momma who was standing in the doorway. "I've gotta whip you little monsters into shape! You have had way too much freedom with those foster parents. Now get ready for bed! And the next time

I tell you to go to your rooms, you had better stay there or else!" "It's only 7 o'clock," protested Thomas. "Shut up! You'll do as you're told you little wimp! And another thing, I will be in my bedroom at the top of the stairs. I can hear anyone who tries to leave. Now move!" We trudged our way into our bedrooms. As I entered mine, she slammed my door shut. I heard 3 more slams after that.

I waited until my watch read 12 o'clock before I dared to make a move. I had passed the time by reading, braiding my hair, and planning the next phase of plan B. Now I was ready. Silently I opened my door. Our momma's door was closed. Hearing no noise, I meowed like a cat. Sarah opened her door and crawled to my room. Without a word Zeke and Thomas came too. I closed the door leaving a small crack to peek through. Since talking would have been suicidal we wrote on a pad of paper. I wrote, Are you ready for the next step? Everyone nodded. I held out my pinkie. We pinkie swore and whispered a phrase I had taught them from the book The Three Musketeers, One for all and all for one! I opened the door. Zeke and Thomas went into their room and closed the door. It creaked. "Who's up," yelled our momma. Sarah and I froze. The bedroom door at the top of the stairs flew open. "What are you doing out of bed Sarah?" "I, I, I," stammered Sarah turning beet red. I thought quickly, "She had a stomachache. She came to me for help." "Why didn't you come to me," demanded Momma looking haughty. I wanted to slap the taste out of her mouth. Instead I answered smoothly, "She didn't want to wake you. But she is fine now. Go to bed Sarah." Sarah gave me a hug and skirted past our momma. After she was safely inside her room I said to Momma as sweetly as I could, "Goodnight." "Huff,' she replied and slammed her door shut. The noise woke up Adam who began to wail, "Mommy! Daddy!" "You better tell him to shut up," growled Momma through her closed door. Sighing, I went to pat Adam back to sleep. Finally I went to bed and fell asleep. It seemed I had barely closed my eyes when I felt a rough shake. "Get up you little heathen! You brats want to wake me up at night so I'm gonna get you up with the early birds!" I sat up and rubbed my eyes and heard her wake up the other kids too. I glanced at my watch. It was 4 o'clock in the morning! "Come on! Don't wake up Adam! I don't want to hear anymore of his whining!" She led us downstairs. On the dining room table were pieces of paper and pencils. Motioning our momma said, "Sit down! The people in that stupid parenting class said that we shouldn't spank you. So they gave us alternative ways to discipline you. Now, I want you write 100 times I will respect my momma at all times. I'm going back to bed." As she turned, Thomas, Sarah, and Naomi began to cry. "Ain't no use in crying. You will just have to learn." Zeke made a face at her retreating back. This caused the kids to laugh and stop crying. We all made faces at the empty staircase and then began to write. Zeke said, "She can make me write it but she can't make me do it." "Don't worry Zeke," I said. "Remember plan B." By the time our momma came back downstairs, we were done and falling asleep. She came over and said loudly, "Good! Now go get dressed while I fix breakfast!" Breakfast was a bowl of cereal and Kool-aid juice. So much for nutrition class! Our momma handed us each a spoon, sat on the couch, and began watching television. Zeke, Sarah, Thomas, Naomi, and I just sat at the table. We didn't eat. We didn't talk. We didn't do a thing. Adam ate his cereal and then sat too. None of us drank our juice. After about 15 minutes had passed, our momma got off of the couch. She was now chatting with her new boyfriend. She turned, saw our full bowls, and said, "I gotta call you back." "Why haven't you eaten your breakfast?" "I'm not hungry," replied Zeke. "Me either," chimed in the rest of us. "Fine! But you won't get anything else until lunch." For lunch she fixed hotdogs, applesauce, and potato chips. Adam ate and then went upstairs for a nap. WE SAT. "Not hungry again? Fine, but you won't get anything until dinnertime." By dinnertime, fish sticks and french fries, she was fed up and starting to get mad. "You'd better eat!" "I'm not hungry," said Zeke smiling. I kicked him under the table and gave him a look that wiped that silly grin clean off his face. "Fine with me,' yelled our momma who stomped over to the couch. By the time we left, I was starving by happy. Phase one of Plan B had begun! The next weekend we continued our food strike. It was easier this time because I had snuck in sandwiches and chips in my overnight bag. Water from the bathroom faucet quenched our thirst. Plan B was successful! We got everyone's attention! Pinchface and Witch #2 were furious! "Starving yourselves isn't going to solve anything," they lectured us. They told all of our parents who agreed with them. "Mary how could you do that," asked Mom. "Did you really think that it would change things?" I told her, "No Mom. But it did get everyone's attention right?" She shook her head and sighed. I sat back and smiled. Now it was time for phase two of Plan B!

Chapter 13

Ironically, phase 2 didn't begin with us. Our momma's boyfriend caused it. We were playing on the floor of the boys' room. He came in and said, "Zeke, Thomas let's play basketball at the park." "We aren't supposed to go without proper supervision," I said. "Shut up Mary! Was I talking to you? Mind your own business! I can supervise them!" "No you can't! And don't be telling my sister to shut up," barked Thomas. "Oh ho little man has some backbone after all," sneered the creep who pushed Thomas causing him to trip and fall over my legs. Quick as a flash Zeke jumped up. He punched the man in the chest and kicked him between his legs! "Don't push my brother you jerk!" Our momma's boyfriend screamed. Our momma flew up the stairs. "What's going on up here?" Her boyfriend began talking rapidly. "Your kids are crazy! That red headed demon kicked me in the nads! That oldest brat can't keep her mouth shut! They are out of control! I'm outta here!" We cheered as we heard "Mr. Wonderful" slam the front door shut. But one look at our momma's face caused Adam to say, "Uh, oh!" He was right. Our momma didn't beat us but we did get locked into our rooms for the rest of the day. On Saturday we couldn't watch television or do anything else. We were only let out of our rooms for meals and scheduled bathroom breaks. After lunch's potty break I whispered, "It's time for Phase 2."

We began to misbehave. It started with small things like kicking the walls and tossing toys. But it quickly grew into outright defiance. We talked back, argued, screamed, and again refused to eat. We were awful! Once again we were lectured by the caseworker, guardian, and our parents. Mom and Dad were really angry this time. They grounded us for 2 whole weeks! But it was worth it. We had successfully gotten everyone's attention again especially our caseworker. Pinchface watched and recorded our behaviors. She knew this game and played it well. Then she made a brilliant move that changed the entire game in our favor. After that 2nd weekend of misbehaving and food strike, we learned that our caseworker, court appointed guardian, and our momma had gone back to court. Witch #2, our guardian, was trying to send us home fast. But this time the judge listened more to our caseworker. I guess her Pinched up facial expression worked on him too! She had explained her continued concern about returning us home too soon. Our food strikes and recent behavior were primary indicators of problems on the horizon if not dealt with now. Witch #2 disagreed. She said that we had been poisoned against our momma by our foster parents. Quick reunification would help us make an easier adjustment. When asked what she thought, our momma sighed heavily and replied, "I don't know. I don't know what the problem is." The judge was intrigued. He said that he wanted to see more data from the visits before making any more decisions. "It's really amazing what you can learn in a hayloft," stated Zeke as he explained all of this to us. We were waiting in a conference room at the visitation center. Our caseworker was running late. We had been placed in the care of a center worker who had stepped outside to have a cigarette. He kept peeking in through the window at us. After 30 minutes passed, Pinchface hurried in. "Come on children." We sighed and picked up our overnight bags. But our gloomy faces changed to surprise when she drove us to a nearby restaurant. After ordering us dinner, she spoke. "I asked your mother for some time alone with you. I wanted to talk to you about your recent behavior. I know what you are up to." She glanced at us not with a pinched look but a smile of amusement. Then she continued, "You tried a food strike and acting naughty. Very clever! Now why don't you try something else?" Without realizing it, all of us kids were leaning forward. She smiled again and said flatly, "Why don't you try acceptance? If you really want to be heard and I'm assuming by your actions that you do, try being good and accepting the situation." By now the food had arrived but no one was eating. Our caseworker continued talking. "I'll tell you a famous quote. It is you can catch more flies with honey than you can with vinegar. You guys have tried vinegar. You got our attention. Now try honey. Be good, help whenever you can, and accept the situation." After saying all of that, she began eating. As we too consumed our food, I thought about what she said. Could she be right? Could simply accepting the situation be our ticket to be heard by the judge? We arrived at our momma's house an hour later. Full of dinner and new ideas we marched bravely into the abode of despair. Before leaving our caseworker hugged each of us and then stated, "Remember, honey not vinegar." We followed her advice. Seeing our total change in behavior our momma sat back and enjoyed the ride. She loved it so much that she let me do the driving. With no more behavioral problems she resumed her old habits. She didn't leave us alone in the house but didn't interact with us. I cooked, cleaned, and cared for the others just as I had before. Our court appointed guardian, Witch #2, attributed our change to our momma's parental skills. "I knew that you could whip them into shape! And it's only been 2 weeks since they were acting up!" Zeke and I glanced at each other and rolled our eyes. What an idiot! Nevertheless, we continued to put our best foot forward confident that we would win over everyone with honey instead of vinegar. We were good. So great in fact that only 3 weeks after that conversation with our caseworker, our guardian came over to our momma's house and announced, "The next court date is in 2 weeks. The judge has heard our reports and will make his final decision. The children will probably be ordered home for good!" She and our momma laughed and chatted away over the news. We, who had been spying since she entered the house, sat in the boys' room in disbelief. "No," cried Naomi. "I don't wanna stay here," cried Thomas. Sarah and Adam began to cry too. Zeke, who didn't say a word, began kicking walls and punching his pillow. The ruckus caused our guardian, our momma, and our caseworker who had just arrived to fly up the staircase. "What's wrong children," asked our caseworker. With every inch of my being, I began screaming, "We want to talk to the judge, now! We want to talk to the judge, now! Now! Now!"

Our caseworker got us a hearing with the judge. Only Zeke, Sarah, Thomas, and I got to speak to him. Naomi and Adam were too young. The judge sat on his bench in a long black robe. He looked mean. He listened to our guardian's report. She suggested that we be sent home immediately. The judge then asked us to stand. Holding hands we all stood bravely and faced him. "Well, children, what do you think about all of this?" I spoke first. "I want to stay with my Mom and Dad. I don't want to go home." "But your Mom and Dad aren't your real parents. They just took care of you for a while." Zeke exclaimed, "They took good care of us! Better than her!" He pointed to our momma who sat in the corner. "Yeah," said Thomas and Sarah. The judge put his hand up and said, "Enough! Bailiff, please take the children outside." We sat in a nearby waiting room. I was elated! For almost 2 years I had waited for someone to ask me what I wanted. Now I had told the judge! Everything was going to be fine now! Our caseworker came into the room. She looked as if she had been crying. Behind her was our guardian. She beamed and gave us the news. "The judge has ordered that you be sent home. You will be going home for good in 2 weeks when you begin your summer vacation."

Chapter 14

The next two weeks were a blur to me. I don't remember anything except for Mom and Dad planning our goodbye party. I had cried so much that my eyes were puffy. Cindy walked around like a zombie. Thomas had vomited after hearing the news. Then he totally stopped eating. He had to be placed in the hospital and was only allowed to leave after Mom and Dad coaxed him to eat a sufficient amount of food to satisfy the doctors. Zeke was also put into the hospital on suicide watch after he tried to runaway, got caught, and threatened, "I'll kill myself before I go live with that woman again!" He was released for the visit after promising to do himself no harm. Sarah stopped talking altogether. She hadn't spoken a word since she left the courthouse. Naomi cried loudly in protest but simply accepted the situation saying, "Well at least we will be together." Adam wasn't told anything because the caseworker felt that he was too young. Mom and Dad bore the news well. They tried to put on a brave front for us. As the first week drew to a close and the Day of Judgment came near I thought that I would die. That weekend we were at our momma's house sitting on the floor in the boy's room. No one spoke. We just sat there looking at the shadows on the wall. Our momma kept checking on us and asking us if we needed anything. For the first time in my life, I saw a look of concern on her face. She called our guardian who rushed right over. We could hear them talking downstairs. "They are just sitting there. What's wrong with them?" "Oh nothing. They will be fine," said our supposed to be guardian. "They just have to adjust to the situation." But she didn't sound convinced. She came upstairs to talk to us. "Now children it won't be so bad. Next week you'll be home for good and have all summer to make new friends." Thomas began to wail loudly. Dad had promised to take him camping this summer. Adam too began crying, "I want my mommy!" Soon we were all crying. Zeke spoke, "I hate you! I hate her! And I hate that Count Dracula judge! I don't want to live here! I want to stay on the farm!" Our guardian began to wring her hands as she glanced at our momma who was now standing in the doorway. "Mary, you are the oldest. Please talk to your brothers and sisters. Tell them that everything will be alright."

"And what do you want me to tell them," I asked with tears streaming down my face. "You want me to lie? You want me to say that even though we followed all of the rules the law failed us! You want me to say that I'm happy to leave the only real home I have had since Gran died? You want me to say that I'm glad to miss my Mom, Dad, and new sister Cindy! You want me to shout for joy at missing girl's camp, swimming lessons, my friends, and more just to come live with an evil woman who feeds us junk and ignores us? What do you want me to say? I don't want to come live here! I have said it a million times! We all have! But nobody cares! Nobody listens! Not Pinchface our caseworker, nor you, you witch, not that idiot judge and especially not our selfish momma who looks and treats us like her personal property! It doesn't matter what I say! In one week you morons are going to end our lives! Here's what I say. I want freedom! I want to be free to make my own choice! That's what I say!" Our caseworker, who arrived shortly before my tirade, was listening. I glanced up as I heard her sobbing and saying, "I'm so sorry." She left for an hour and returned to take us back to the visitation center. We hugged each other and said tearful goodbyes. We knew that the next time we came together would be the day our caseworker would bring us to our momma's house for good. Little did we know the game wasn't over yet.

Our caseworker called her supervisor that night. She told him that something had to be done about the Smith case and fast. By Wednesday of the following week, Thomas was back in the hospital. He stopped eating again. Our caseworker and guardian came with us to visit him at the hospital. "What did the doctor say," Pinchface asked Mom who was sitting beside Thomas' bed and stroking his head. Mom looked up and replied, "The doctor said that Thomas was in shock. Only time and rest will help him now." I walked over to her and gave her a hug. "Don't cry Mom. It's just like you have been telling us. It will all work out in the end." Our caseworker spoke, "It has been the same with all of the children. We have visited everyone and all of the children are having similar reactions." She told us about her home visits. Adam had been screaming and throwing tantrums all day. His foster mom had informed him that morning that soon he would be living with our momma and us. She didn't want it to be a surprise and thought that by telling him the truth she could better prepare him for the transition. That proved to be a huge mistake. Adam became hysterical. He vomited from crying so hard and could only be comforted when his foster mom held him. At the next house, our caseworker found Naomi sitting in her living room on her foster mom's lap. She too had cried and threw tantrums all week. The only solace for her was a song that her foster mom sang to her and cuddling with her bear. At Sarah's house, our caseworker was dumbstruck to find Sarah sitting facing a wall and stroking her dog. Her foster Mom and Dad explained that she still wouldn't talk and ate very little. She allowed herself to be dressed and then would sit facing the wall petting the family dog that growled whenever Pinchface tried to get near Sarah. As bad as everyone was, Zeke was the worst. He repeated his threat of killing himself. When our guardian told him that such talk could land him back in the hospital, he shut his mouth. He didn't want to lose any time with the "Ingalls". Unfortunately, he then got it into his head that maybe a hospital stay was better than going to live with our momma. So he tried to injure himself. He jumped off the hayloft but found that the years on the farm had strengthened and toughened him up. So he jumped off the barn roof. He ended up breaking his arm. After that he was done, not because he wanted to be but because his foster Dad told him, "You try anymore of that nonsense again Zachariah Smith and I will personally deliver you to your momma's house!" We, our caseworker explained, were the last stop. As she and our guardian prepared to leave, I heard Pinchface say, "I wonder if things will truly work out after all."

Chapter 15

By Friday morning I was a complete emotional and mental wreck. Our last day of school had been the previous day. Everyone said goodbye and entered their summer vacation with glee. I stepped into mine as if I were walking towards the electric chair. I knew that the next day was Doomsday. Thomas was still in the hospital. For a while we thought that Sarah would join him. Her doctor was worried about her mental state and wanted to place her in the psych ward for observation. But our guardian said to wait and see. Adam's foster dad got him to calm down by getting him a puppy after our momma agreed that the dog could come too. Naomi's foster parents took her to an amusement park and promised to do so again for each of her birthdays. This too our momma agreed to. Zeke's foster father promised Zeke a horse when he was grown if he obeyed and did well in school. He even bought Zeke a new saddle to take along to remind him of his promise. Of course with Thomas in the hospital, Mom, Dad, Cindy, and I didn't feel like celebrating. Mom promised that once Thomas got well we would have a party at their house and all of our brothers and sisters could come. Our momma had agreed to do this. I sat in Thomas' room thinking that if our momma could agree to all of these things, why couldn't she agree to let us go? I glanced at Thomas who had fallen asleep. I sighed and wondered if his illness was a blessing in disguise. The doctors refused to allow him to leave based on his medical condition. I wonder…As I pondered this, Dad rushed into the room. He whispered something to Mom who nodded and quickly walked over to me. "Mary we have to go!" "But I want to stay with Thomas!" "Dad and Cindy will be here. Now come on!" Mom had never yelled before! I climbed into the van, buckled my seatbelt, and glanced sideways at Mom, "You and Dad aren't going to kidnap me and Thomas and run are you?" Mom laughed, "No honey. It's nothing like that. Just wait." We drove to the courthouse. "Why are we here?" "You'll see."

As I walked into a large conference room that Mom pointed to, I saw Zeke, Sarah, Naomi, and Adam sitting with Pinchface, our guardian, our momma, a court reporter, and 2 police officers. We children sat across a large table facing the adults. No one made a sound as I glared at the people who I felt had completely ruined my life. What did they want now? The judge walked in without his black robe. Zeke leaned over and whispered, "He must have left his robe in his casket." The judge, who had overhead him, smiled and said, "Well this is quite a turnout! Everybody raise your hand!" He swore us to tell the truth and then spoke again, "I understand that there have been some interesting developments in this case. I want to know about them. But first why don't the children go with Mr. Stanton." He motioned to a man who I hadn't noticed standing in a corner. When none of us moved, the judge said to me, "It's ok Mary. He is your caseworker's boss." I nodded slowly and took Adam's hand. We followed Mr. Stanton to the judge's chambers. He gave us some paper and crayons but we just sat there. What was going on? Zeke turned to Mr. Stanton and asked, "Are you really Pinchface's boss?" I smacked him in the back of his head and hissed, "Shut up stupid! We are in enough trouble already!" Mr. Stanton laughed as Zeke rubbed his head. "Yes I am." Zeke stood up and moved away from my range. "I think that you ought to fire her! She's lousy!" The man cracked up as I stood up and said, "Zachariah Smith sit down and be quiet or I'll strangle you!" At that moment the judge walked in with the court reporter. He said cheerfully, "Please sit down children. I would like to talk to you." We sat on the floor with him and stared at him with wide eyes. He continued, "I have heard a lot about all of you including your brother Thomas who isn't here." He looked at Adam who had climbed onto my lap. "I hear that you have a new puppy. Is that right?" Adam smiled and said, "Yep! My Daddy gave him to me! He's brown and housebroke too!" "Your daddy gave him to you?" Adam looked at him funny. "Yeah, I live with Mommy and Daddy." The judge smiled and asked, "Don't you want to live with your momma?" Adam screwed up his face and began screaming, "No! I want my Mommy! I want my Daddy!" I gave the judge a dirty look as he motioned to Mr. Stanton. He picked up Adam and carried him to the door. I stood to follow but stopped when I saw Adam's' foster mom reached out and take him. I sat back down as the judge turned to Naomi and gently tugged on one of her ponytails. "How old are you sweetheart?" Naomi smiled and answered, "I'm 7 years old." "Do you know what a lie is?" "It's when you don't tell the truth. My mommy says to always tell the truth." "Your momma that you go visit?" Naomi frowned and said sullenly, "No, not her! My real mommy!" The judge then turned to Sarah. She had followed us meekly into the judge's chambers, parked herself on the floor and not moved or spoken. The judge said, "Sarah, Sarah, look at me please sweetheart." But Sarah continued to sit. The only moment she made was to blink every so often. The judge wiped his face on his hand and spoke to Zeke. "How did you break your arm young man?" "I fell." "You fell or jumped?" "Alright! I jumped off the barn roof!" "Why? You are old enough to know better than that!" "I do know better." "Well then why did you do it?" Zeke glanced away for a minute. I could see that he was fighting back tears. "I don't know anymore," he sobbed. He wiped the tears away and spoke again. "I just don't want to go live with that woman!" "And you thought that jumping off the roof would stop that?" Zeke shook his head. "No. But look at Thomas. He's not here because he's in the hospital. I just wanted to go anywhere else instead of that house!" He patted his cast and hung his head with a deep sigh. The judge sighed too and finally turned towards me. I had been listening to everyone. Each time someone spoke I went to them, stood by them as the judge address them, and hugged them when he was done. I was patting Zeke's back now. The judge looked at me and smiled. "You are going to make a great mom someday Mary. I guess things were really tough when you lived with your momma, especially on you." I nodded and sat down next to Zeke. "But things changed when I went to live with Mom, Dad, and Cindy." "Did they tell you to call them that?" "No. Thomas and I talked about it one day and just decided to." "But don't you love your momma?" I thought carefully before I answered. "I guess I do. But it's different." "How?" "Well she really wasn't a mother to me. After Gran died I had to be the momma. She didn't even try. Now she hates me because all of the kids look to me and not her. My mom, the one I live with, is the only other real mom I've had except for Gran. She cooks, cleans, sews, and does all of the mother things. I don't have to." The judge nodded and asked, "Mary, tell me truthfully. What do you want to happen?" I looked him straight in the eye and boldly stated, "I want to stay with my family, my Mom and Dad! We all do!"

The judge left after speaking to me. Adam came back in the room with our caseworker. We looked out of the windows of the judge's office. Time passed slowly. Mr. Stanton brought us some food to eat. We picked at it but really didn't enjoy it. The McDonald's that normally made us happy seemed like a last meal before execution. "When are they going to let us out," asked Zeke who was pacing the floor. "Soon honey," said Pinchface who had been trying in vain to get Sarah to eat. The shadows on the wall changed. After leading Sarah to the bathroom, I glanced at my watch. It was almost 6 o'clock. The door of the office swung open... Our guardian walked in. "Mary, the judge would like to see you." I marched out of the room and followed her down the hall. I could hear my heartbeat pounding as it drummed the death march song. As I entered the conference room that we had previously been in, I saw the judge, my momma, and the court reporter. Panic gripped me. What was this? Oh, no! Here it comes! Bravely, I squared my shoulders and faced the firing squad. "Mary," the judge began. Ready, aim... "I have decided that you don't have to go." I opened my eyes. "What?" The judge smiled and repeated, "I decided that you, your brothers, and sisters don't have to go. You can stay with your foster parents. You will still have weekly visits at the visitation center. I think that this is what's best for everyone." I stood there staring blankly. We could stay! We didn't have to leave! I glanced at my momma who stood and said, "I want you kids to be happy. It's all I've ever wanted." Then she sat down and cried. I walked over to her and said, "Don't cry Momma." She looked up, smiled and hugged me tight. That was the first time any of us had called her Momma since we had been removed 2 years before. "Let's go tell your brothers and sisters," suggested the judge. I walked towards him and nodded. Then I stopped and turned towards our momma. "Thanks."

Chapter 16

Of course you would think that this is the end. We all lived happily ever after. Wrong! I told you that bad luck follows Lydia Anne Smith and unfortunately her children too. True to his word, the judge let us stay with our foster parents. When we told the other children the news, they screamed and danced for joy. Sarah who hadn't spoken for almost 2 weeks whispered, "I can stay with my Mommy and Daddy?" It was as if someone had turned on a light switch. Thomas too seemed to wake out of a trance. He began eating, responded well to the therapy sessions ordered by the judge for us all, and was released from the hospital in time for our first visit 2 weeks later. The visit was a happy occasion with everyone in attendance including our former caseworker who we renamed Grace. We learned that she had made several phone calls that led to the final meeting with the judge. Our momma may have seemed to lose the game but she wasn't' through playing yet. She moved into a one bedroom apartment, dyed her hair, and came to the visits when they suited her. She seemed to be enjoying her new life. But she wouldn't allow us to be adopted. The judge stated very clearly that if she missed 3 visits in a row, her rights would be terminated. When we asked our caseworker what that meant, she explained that it meant we would be free to be adopted by our parents. Of course, our momma wasn't going to let that happen. When I questioned her about it she said, "Look Mary, I let you stay where you are. But you are my kids!" So she made her moves. She would miss one visit and come the next 2 weeks. Or she would miss 2 in a row and be sure to make the next one. No one could stop her because she followed the rules. Even though we all became frustrated by her reckless actions and complained bitterly, the judge stood by his ruling. He wouldn't terminate our momma's parental rights unless she violated his previous judgment. We tried to convince our momma to allow us to be adopted. We promised to write, call, and visit her. "No! You are my kids!" The constant bickering began to wear on her. She got thinner. She missed more and more visits getting dangerously close to 3 in a row.

Then one day Mom and Dad came into the den where Thomas, Cindy, and I were playing Monopoly. "Cindy and Thomas please go to your rooms. We would like to talk to Mary." After they left, Mom said, "Mary we have some bad news to tell you. Your momma is in the hospital." "What for?" Dad answered, "The doctors aren't exactly sure what's wrong. They say that she's worn out, exhausted, and malnourished. Apparently she has been living a hard life lately." I nodded. "She's been fighting against everyone including herself." Mom smiled and hugged me. "Mary, you are one smart cookie for such a young age! Your wisdom amazes me!" The visits stopped because our momma was too ill to attend. Grace had visited her several times in the hospital and tried to convince her to sign the consent forms releasing us to be adopted by our foster families that we have lived with for more than 2 years. But our momma refused. "I love them. I can't let them go!" I went to see her one late Sunday afternoon. She was hooked up to a lot of machines. She looked awful. "Hello Momma." She opened her eyes and smiled. "Mary!" "How are you?" "I'm tired Mary," she said with a faraway look in her eyes. "You saved my life the day you born. Did you know that? I was ready to give up until I held you for the first time. I named you Mary to remind me of her Son Jesus Who saved us all. You, all of you kids, have been my world, my life." Tears formed in my eyes. "I know Momma. And you loved us." "Yes," she said quietly. "But I didn't always show it, did I?" I walked over to her bed and said, "You still can Momma. You can sign the papers. You can set us free!" She looked at me briefly and shook her head. "No, I can't!" "Why not?"

She tried to sit up. Too weary she leaned back and replied, "I promised Mary. I promised Gran that I would never give any of you away! I promised that I would never do that! I told her that I would die before that happened!" She looked at me again this time with tears streaming down her thin, pale face. "You see Mary. I told you that you were only half right. I did know you. All of you kids are my promise to your Gran, my only link to her! I never broke that promise. Even when they took all of you away, I did everything they said to see you and get you back together. I kept my promise!" Exhausted, she closed her eyes. I patted her hand and kissed her cheek. "You kept your promise Momma. Gran would be proud of you." She died 2 days later.

So here we are: Zeke now 13, Sarah now 12, Thomas almost 11, Naomi age 9, Adam age 7, and me almost 16 standing by our momma's black casket on this rainy day. We were free! Our moms and dads sat behind us. Also in attendance were our former supervisor, guardian, and the judge. We children huddled together as the minister read on. When he finished, the rain abruptly stopped. The sun began to peek out from behind a cloud. Adam yelled, "Look!" Everyone turned and let out a collective gasp. A beautiful rainbow was in the sky! One by one our parents came over to us. They all had recently filed adoption papers on us. They agreed that the six of us could visit once a month. We could call and write as often as we liked. We would always be our momma's kids, brothers and sisters together, forever! I glanced again at the colorful arc in the sky. Then I turned towards my siblings. We were as different and variously arrayed as that rainbow. Just before it completely faded away, I said to the assembled mass, "Momma's happy now! She kept her promise after all!"

Epilogue

That was years ago. I am a mother of 6 children now. My husband is a doctor who cares for the elderly just as my own father had. Three of our children are adopted. My only daughter, my firstborn, is named Lydia Anne. Zachariah a.k.a. Zeke married and lives on his own farm. He raises horses starting with the one his dad promised him. Zeke also has 3 fiery red headed sons of his own. Sarah became a dancer for a ballet theater troop. She has traveled all over the world. Although she is a stunning beauty, she has yet to get married. Thomas always had weak health. I suppose that was why he became a pediatrician. He and his wife have 4 kids including a son named Scott after our father and a daughter named Mary. Naomi married and lives with her husband in Los Angeles where she is a practicing attorney. Little Adam grew up to be a teacher like his adopted mother. He lives a quiet life in the country with his grown up puppy Max. Every Mother's Day we put flowers on our momma's grave. We tell her how we are doing and then spend the rest of the day together reminiscing with each other. It's like having those visits all over again! One day I was cleaning out my attic when I found two very old, worn books. One was Heidi and the other was A Little Princess. When I opened Heidi, I saw an inscription written inside. It read: Mary remember that life may be tough, but things will improve. Always, your 6th grade Spanish teacher Mrs. Ramos. Smiling I opened the second book. In it I found an inscription that I knew from memory. It read: Life has its ups and downs. It has its highs and lows. But without falling down one can't look up. Without the lows we wouldn't be able to appreciate and enjoy the highs. Always remember that you are a princess no matter what happens. Love, Aunt Lucy a.k.a. Mom. I held the books in my arms and whispered, "I promise."